Murder at the Mansion

A Cornish Witch Mystery

Stella Berry

If you would like to be informed immediately when future books by this author are released then visit the website www.stellaberrybooks.com

This book was written and edited in the UK, where some spelling, grammar and word usage will vary from US English

Dedicated to my Grandmother
Your talent passed down.
And your stories of growing up in our version of
Latheborne Manor
Bleak realities and all!
You are missed.

Contents

Prologue

Judy checked her husband was sleeping before slipping out of bed. She'd not really expected him to come to their room until the early hours and had been concerned that his presence was going to interfere with her plans. But he'd taken the sleeping pills like a lamb, without even knowing it. Just a small dose, not enough to kill, not even enough to keep him asleep if she wasn't quiet. But she'd wanted to be careful, after all, it was all for him.

She crept up along the corridor, checking around her all the time. She wasn't scared, but more anxious not to be witnessed and draw suspicion.

She got a slight shiver as she began to ascend the stairs up to the music room. Foreboding or anticipation? She wasn't sure which; probably anticipation. Knowledge was power, and she did so like having the power to elevate or destroy at her whim.

She pushed open the door to the music room and let out a shriek as something small and furry rushed past her in the dark. She put a hand to her chest, just a cat. There was no one else, she was here first, ready to trap her next victim.

It wasn't until she felt the breath on the back of her neck that she realised she'd made a terrible mistake…

Chapter One

Morgana stared at the telephone hardly able to believe what her twin sister was asking of her.

"You want me to pretend to be you? For a whole weekend, surrounded by your work colleagues? Are you mad?"

"They're not my work colleagues. Only one of them has actually ever met me. Bernie Gossard, the Director, and he's not going to be paying any attention at all, there will be far more important people than me that he has to talk to." Morwenna sounded like it was paining her to be patient. "It's a house party, in a posh mansion, where the film is going to be set. That's all. Just the director of the movie, a couple of big stars, some money-bags I'm supposed to be sweet to, and their other halves. That's it. Ten people at most. All you need to do is show up, be charming, eat, drink, sleep, and go home again!"

"Be charming?" Morgana raised an eyebrow. "You're never charming. It would be a total giveaway when they met the real you."

"I could be nice, if necessary, and if it landed me a role in a genuine Hollywood movie! But you're right, you do charm so much better than I could anyway." Morwenna's tone turned wheedling. "This is the most important opportunity of my career, Morgana, I have to be seen to be there."

"Then be there," Morgana said, confused.

"I can't! Didn't you hear what I said? It's the same weekend my boyfriend's mother has asked to meet me."

Morgana lay back on her squashy sofa and put a cushion behind her head. She could tell this conversation was going to go on a great deal longer than she'd like if she wanted to understand what was going on with Morwenna.

"New boyfriend, yes, I understood that bit. Love of your life, yadda yadda, but when have you ever cared what their mother's thought?"

"Since I was summoned to Court by Queen Esme of Piama."

"Queen what of the what now? How is this relevant?"

"She's his mother!" Morwenna yelled in exasperation.

Morgana held the phone away from her ear and looked at it balefully as Morwenna's voice continued to shout in her ear.

"His mother is Queen Esme, you half-wit. She wants to meet me and if I say I'm too busy, or my career is more important, then he's never going to be allowed to marry me. I can't snub her by not going and I can't turn down the weekend at the mansion either or my part in the film will go to someone else. How are you not getting this?"

"Wait." Morgana rubbed at her tired head. "Your boyfriend is a Prince? Like, real royalty?"

"Yes!" Morwenna lowered her voice almost to a hiss.

"So…You'll be Queen of Pepperoni one day if you marry him?"

"Piama, and no, he's not the eldest son. He's only third in line to the throne, and his brother's wife is pregnant, so possibly fourth in line. That really isn't the point, Mog. The point is that his mum is the potential mother-in-law from hell, and I don't want to tick her off, at least not until we're married."

"You really think you'll marry the pepperoni prince?" Morgana only said this to annoy her sister. Morwenna needed teasing on this crazy idea, that was for sure. "You have been engaged several times already, and they've all fallen through."

Morwenna expelled a long breath of irritation. "Morgana, I'm asking you for help. I've never asked you for much, but I'm in a bind. I can't be in both places at once, but, lucky for me I have an identical double. What do you say? Will you be a sport and pretend to be me for three short days? The place is only forty minutes drive away, it's a stunning Elizabethan manor house, there will be food, and drinks, and entertainment, and you just have to smile and tell everyone how marvellous they are and then come home again. Easy as pie."

Morgana considered it. It might be rather fun to pretend to be Morwenna. To stop caring what people thought and just be as wild as she pleased. Morwenna had a flair for the dramatic that Morgana had often secretly envied. Her clothes, her caustic wit, her flamboyant gestures. It would be playing a part that she knew very well but had never really had the nerve to pull off as herself.

"You're sure nobody else there has actually met you? No one is going to ask me to remember some great night when you went home with them and did indecent things?" She asked suspiciously.

"Absolutely not. I'll give you a detailed list of everyone who's coming. I know all there is to know about all of them. These people are all already up there,

American A-list. I'm the nobody local girl who can lend authenticity to a British production. I'm not playing a lead, just the 'best friend' character. Bernie Gossard invited me, he saw me perform in Othello and loved me, but it's not the Director I'm there to impress. He wants me to be suck up to a man called Dickie Magnus."

"That's never his real name?" Morgana said with a giggle.

"No idea. Probably. Anyway, Dickie is the money behind the movie. He's supposed to be wowed by the 'historical' location and made to feel like the big tamale. More importantly, he has a weakness for redheads and for Scottish whisky, and posh British crumpet."

"I'm not any of those things," Morgana pointed out.

"You will be. My hair has red low lights right now, so you'll need to add those, and so long as you don't go all Cornish *Ooh Arr* on him, then you can sound posh enough to pass muster. He's American, he won't know the difference."

Morgana scowled and lifted a chunk of her hair to examine it. It was dark brown and she liked it that way. Dying it red seemed like a step too far.

"This is a huge favour you're asking from me. I do have a business to run," she sniped.

"It's November. Your shop is quiet as the grave right now, and don't even bother to pretend it isn't, I know Portmage is a ghost town at this time of year. Would it really matter if you took a few itty bitty days off?" Morwenna was back to wheedling.

Morgana silently conceded that her sister was right, even if she didn't voice it. Her hometown was a tourist destination all summer long, with its windswept beaches and the ancient castle. But come colder months, the crowds returned to the city and her little shop was empty a great deal of the time. It wouldn't make a huge difference if she took a couple of days off. In fact, quite a lot of the local businesses shut up for the entire winter season.

"Fine, I'll play at being the wicked one for a weekend. But you owe me."

"I'll make it up to you, I swear. When I'm a Princess I shall bestow some honour upon you, a national holiday in your name or something." Morwenna promised fervently.

Morgana snorted, but the deal was done. "You have to give me every detail, Mew, every tiny detail about these people!"

"Oh totes," Morwenna agreed enthusiastically. "But honestly, they are all so self-involved, none of them are going to pay the slightest attention to you. Easy as pie."

"Right," Morgana agreed her tone heavy with sarcasm. "What could possibly go wrong?"

Chapter Two

Two weeks later, Morgana had packed her most trashy-classy *Morwenna-ish* clothes, streaked her hair, painted her normally bare nails a deep wine red, and swapped her pentacle necklace for opals. The opals were probably still too witchy for Morwenna to ever wear, but at least they were genuine and genuinely expensive. She had a feeling this crowd would recognise fake jewels even if they didn't recognise fake personalities.

Her sister wasn't 'out' about being a witch: she always said that theatre people were too superstitious to handle it, so Morgana had also hidden her large amethyst crystal in a velvet pouch which she'd then tucked into her bra. She was going to need it on this trip!

Latheborne Manor was situated right in the middle of Dartmoor. The entire area was National Parkland and Morgana would have been hard pushed to find anywhere more bleak and isolated. The long winding road to reach the property had been populated only by the occasional sheep and tufts of grass that were the single thing that thrived there. She'd passed no houses for many miles, no villages, and no other traffic for at least the last twenty minutes. The manor might only be a forty-minute drive from Portmage, but it felt like a million miles from the seaside resort she called home. This was in-land, and yet more remote than any island. Huge wrought iron gates, set in a high stone that circled away in both directions, stood open and she drove through them feeling as though she were entering a hidden world. She was extremely grateful for her old Land Rover, as she bumped along the pitted drive and swerved to avoid some of the bigger potholes. Its huge tyres were unintimidated by the terrain, and she wondered how a sports car would fare.

Morgana began to suspect, judging by the state of the drive, that the owner of Latheborne Manor was probably in need of a cash influx to maintain the upkeep of the place. Which explained why they had allowed their home to be used as a film set.

She rounded a bend and got her first view of the house, feeling surprise and admiration go through her at the sight of it. It was predominantly built in the typical style of the Georgian era. A big block of a building made to withstand the elements, with high chimneys and tall windows, and a single gothic tower poking up at the back. The front door was set forward and stood between two Doric columns, and, as her noisy car drew close, the door opened.

Morgana took a moment to close her eyes and reinforce her protective charms. She needed all her barriers up to deal with an entire weekend of close proximity with strangers. She curled her fingers around her hidden crystal and centred herself, dampening down all her empathic abilities so she didn't have to deal with anyone's emotions but her own.

Being psychic to auras and the strong feelings of anyone around her was much more of a curse than a gift when surrounded by strangers. With her wards firmly in place, she opened her eyes and looked toward the house, seeing two men stepping out of the front door.

The first man was familiar. She recognised him as he lifted a hand, shading his eyes against the afternoon sunshine. It was the director, Bernie Gossard. She'd looked him up on the internet after her conversation with Morwenna, and the pictures helped her with her quick identification.

He was tall, lean, and in his early fifties. His hair was already silver, but it suited him, and he was deeply tanned. He looked every inch like a Colonial just back from the Far East, complete with the Panama hat, that just managed to stay put despite the breeze in the November air.

The other man, however, was a mystery to her. Equally straight-backed, but in his mid-thirties. He wore tan corduroy trousers and a thick navy blue woollen jumper, that looked far more suited to the cold weather, and he seemed to glare at her with arrogant eyes as though she had insulted him already.

She parked carefully beside a range rover and was just pulling her suitcase from the boot of her car as Bernie came down the steps to greet her.

"Morwenna, darling," he said enthusiastically. For a second she thought he was about to hug her, but he placed a hand on her arm, leaned forward, and kissed the air just inches from each of her cheeks.

She mimicked the gesture, hugely relieved. It might all be normal for the real Morwenna, but Morgana valued her personal space and found the intimacy of the greeting slightly uncomfortable. She wasn't naturally a physically affectionate person with anyone except family.

You're just going to have to get used to it, she silently scolded herself.

"How wonderful that you're here so early, I genuinely appreciate it," Bernie said, earnestly.

Morgana looked at her watch in surprise. "I'm sorry,

I thought I was supposed to be here at four?" It was five minutes past four.

Bernie gave an indulgent laugh. "Absolutely right, m'dear. Though I think it's highly unlikely any of the others will bother to show before five. You know how these types are."

Morgana tried not to grind her teeth. This was the sort of detail that Morwenna would have known, but she didn't.

He drew her toward the front door where the second man waited. "Allow me to introduce you both. My Lord, this is Morwenna Emrys, a talented ingénue, and the toast of London for her portrayal of Desdemona on the West End this summer. Morwenna, may I present Lord Oliver Westley, Baron of Latheborne."

Morgana wasn't sure whether she was supposed to curtsey or something to a Lord, so she settled for inclining her head respectfully to him before lifting her face to meet his eyes. She hadn't been wrong about the arrogant stare, but the disapproval she saw there was something of a shock. His look was almost one of loathing.

Morwenna, what did you fail to tell me about this one? She thought in dismay. There was no way he could dislike her so much if they had no history.

For a second they locked eyes and he let her see exactly how little he thought of her, and then the expression was wiped away and he stepped forward with a coolly polite smile. "Welcome to my home, Miss Emrys."

She couldn't help but notice in that moment, how much his dark blue eyes were an exact match for the navy blue of his jumper. They were like the sea in the evening. Icy cold, but with deep depths.

He didn't extend his hand or try to greet her with any of the warmth shown by Bernie, he simply stood and waited for her response.

"Have we met before, Lord Latheborne?" she asked, desperately hoping that she wasn't ruining everything before she'd even started.

"We have not," he confirmed.

She gave him a confused look, wondering why he was so down on Morwenna if she hadn't even met him until now.

"But I believe you know my nephew rather well, Ethan Cope?"

"Oh, right, of course." Morgana tried to look as unphased as possible by this unforeseen connection. Did Morwenna really know Ethan Cope? Even Morgana had heard of him, despite her lack of film knowledge. Ethan Cope was the hottest property coming out of England for the past two years, in more ways than one. He was young, gorgeous, talented, and had played Charles Darwin in a recent role that had gained him an Oscar at the age of only twenty-one. "Lovely chap," she added lamely.

He raised a sardonic brow. "Lovely? What an unusual adjective to choose. Capricious and ubiquitously glib would be a more common elucidation."

Morgana ground her teeth. She was going to have to watch herself around this one.

The only question that now remained was whether Lord Latheborne so strongly disapproved of her because she was an actress, or because she knew his nephew, or for some reason she'd yet to fathom.

Chapter Three

"It's very good of you to have us all," she said, changing the subject away from his nephew, and making a mental note to chew Morwenna out the second she got a moment alone to call her.

"And it's good of you to arrive on time. Punctuality seems to be a forgotten art these days," he replied equally.

She gave a small smile. "Oh well, the early bird catches the worm and all that."

"Indeed." The coldness reappeared in his blue eyes. "Just don't get confused about who the worm is." He turned and led the way inside.

Morgana clenched her jaw. What exactly did he mean by that? That he expected her to try and seduce him? She'd certainly done nothing to give him that impression, if you didn't count admiring the colour of his eyes, of course. No, he must have heard something about Morwenna that made him think that. Well, he was going to be disappointed. So far, she thought he was nothing but a cold fish with a stick up his handsome backside.

She followed the two men into the house. As she stepped into the entrance hall she stopped and allowed her eyes to travel upwards. The entire foyer was as big as her shop and the flat above it combined. It stretched upwards three floors if she counted the ground floor where she currently stood. A balcony circled three sides where the stairs reached the first floor, and again where they reached the second. From her position on the ground floor, it felt dizzying to look up. She imagined it was probably less intimidating if you were looking down, but you still wouldn't want to lean over the wooden banister rail which was all that protected you from the drop.

She looked down as something brushed against her foot, stepping hastily backward to avoid tripping over the head of a gigantic tiger skin on the floor.

"It's not real," Lord Latheborne said, with almost a smile. "My great grandfather shot the original in India, but when he returned home his dogs took great exception to the skin and mauled it beyond repair. So, he had a replica made that didn't seem to bother them quite so much."

Morgana, who hated anyone wearing fur, was about to comment on how smart the dogs were, but decided to bite her tongue instead and settled for something non-committal.

"How unfortunate."

Clearly her bland comment still managed to annoy Lord Latheborne, because he gave her a withering look in response.

"Well, I love it," Bernie declared. "It adds authenticity even if it isn't."

Morgana frowned over this but decided that this time, silence was the most prudent response.

"In that case, I think you should have it when you're done filming," Lord Latheborne said, giving the older man a wry glance. "I've only left it there because you said you liked it, I hate the thing myself. I keep meaning to have a big clear out now I'm back."

He went up slightly in Morgana's estimation at these words, though not a lot, particularly as there was also a stags head over the door at the rear of the room, and she was pretty sure that was real.

"Louise?" Lord Latheborne yelled suddenly, making her jump.

A girl of about eighteen appeared at the top of the stairs. She wore skinny jeans, with designer rips in them, and a tank top over a shirt.

"You called?" she said, leaning against the balcony.

"Can you take Miss Emrys' luggage up to the Primrose Room?" He gestured at the case in Morgana's hand.

Morgana's eyebrows went up. She'd thought the girl was a guest, judging by her relaxed attitude. But she now noticed the dusting cloth in her hands and realised she must be a housemaid, despite her lack of formal dress. That was another pleasant surprise. Lord Latheborne might be a peer of the realm, but he didn't make his staff wear ridiculous outdated outfits.

Louise sauntered down and took the case from Morgana, who debated protesting and then decided not to.

"It's up one floor, third on the right," Louise said. "Just in case you were wondering."

Morgana gave her a grateful nod and skirted around the rug continuing to follow the men as they entered a door to the right, and found herself in a grand room. A fire burned in the heath beneath a huge marble mantle and a few armchairs and a chaise were set around it.

"This is the formal Drawing Room," Lord Latheborne told her. "It's not used a great deal these days, except when we occasionally hire the place out for weddings. Couples seem to like it for photos and so forth. Bernie thought it would be a suitable place for all the guests to meet and gather."

"It's very… impressive," Morgana said, feeling that the room had a chill to it, despite the roaring fire.

"I've always found it rather cold and unwelcoming," Lord Latheborne said, more to himself than to her.

Morgana watched an ethereal figure float straight through the closed door at the far end and bend over to tend the fire. The fire sputtered in response and the flames diminished slightly.

"It's probably because of the ghost," she commented.

Lord Latheborne looked startled and Morgana silently cursed herself. But then a knowing smile touched his lips. "You've done your research on the place, I see."

Morgana decided to avoid answering that, and, as soon as the ghost was done, she moved over to the fire to warm her hands over it.

"My wife, Judy, will be down in a moment, Morwenna. She's looking forward to meeting you." Bernie looked out the window to the driveway, clearly anticipating the arrival of the other guests.

"There's also my grandmother, who is currently napping in the parlour. No doubt she'll join us as soon as the drinks come out, so perhaps we should get some on the go?" Lord Latheborne suggested, moving past Morgana and pulling a long velvet sash that hung to one side of the fireplace.

Morgana raised her brows at him, humour dancing in her eyes. It was just such a very old fashioned way to summon a servant.

Lord Latheborne gave a rueful smile in return,

immediately catching her meaning. "A staff of just three. There's no way I could manage the cleaning of this place without the housekeeper and the maid, and my housekeeper is also a fantastic cook, for which I'm very grateful considering the number of guests this weekend."

"You don't keep a chef?" Bernie asked, in apparent surprise.

Lord Latheborne gave a shrug. "It's just me most of the time, and my grandmother prefers simple food. Besides, I'm used to fending for myself. It would be embarrassing all round if I kept someone just to make me a sandwich. I assume you bring catering vans when you make a movie?"

Bernie nodded, then brightened as a formal looking butler appeared in the door pushing a drinks trolley before him.

Morgana blinked with surprise at the butler. For some reason, she had expected a decrepit old man, with white hair and a foreboding expression. Instead, the butler was young, gorgeous, and very camp. She cast a curious glance at Lord Latheborne wondering if the butler was more than just a butler to him. Lord Latheborne looked to be somewhere in his mid-thirties and the butler was probably around twenty-five, so it wasn't inconceivable by any stretch.

The young man grinned at Morgana. "What would you like, Miss Emrys? I have wine, sherry, and a selection of spirits or I can mix any cocktail."

A smile spread across Morgana's face. The butler might be young but he was clearly good at his job, and he probably had a fair idea of the kind of crowd he'd be serving.

She glanced at her watch and decided that the hour was late enough to merit alcohol. Plus, she might need it to get through meeting everyone else, just so long as she stayed on the ball enough not to say anything stupid and give the game away.

"Just a brandy, I think, to take the chill off," she said.

"Make that two," Lord Latheborne concurred.

"Martini for me," Bernie said as the butler looked towards him questioningly. "Make that two as well, I can see my wife on her way down."

"And my grandmother I suspect. Probably heard the clinking of the bottles by now," Lord Latheborne muttered to himself. Morgana realised she wasn't supposed to have heard him and managed to suppress her giggle as a cough. Lord Latheborne, however, must have noticed, because he shot her a guilty look and they shared a smile. A second later the moment of warmth was gone from his eyes as though he had just remembered that he didn't like her.

Brandy with disapproval for one, Morgana thought with a grimace.

"Judy, come and meet Morwenna," Bernie said, as a woman came into the room.

Judy Gossard was also not at all what Morgana had been expecting. She'd decided quite quickly that Bernie had an eye for the ladies, and had expected either an exceedingly glamorous older wife or a young and stunning second wife. Judy was neither. She looked middle-aged and *fluffy*. Plump, and in a flowery dress, she was soft and feminine in a motherly way. Her auburn hair was curled and streaked with grey, which she made no effort to hide. She surveyed the room with a vaguely scatty air and would have given off an immediate impression of warm absentmindedness but for the steel in her eyes.

She sees everything and pretends to see nothing, Morgana thought, whimsically.

"So, you're the new actress that Bernie says has real potential," Judy said, giving Morgana a very thorough once over as she accepted her drink.

"Not new to acting, but only on stage so far," Morgana said, playing the part of her sister. "I'm flattered that your husband thinks I have potential."

"He doesn't say it to be flattering, you must be genuinely good or he wouldn't have chosen you."

"Thank you." Morgana couldn't help feeling proud of her sister at the sincerity of the other woman's pronouncement.

"I like you," Judy said, decisively. "I wasn't sure I would, but now I've seen you, I know I do. I can always tell."

Morgana gave her a shrewd look. Judy was obviously excellent at reading people. She'd bet her hat that her sister wouldn't have fared nearly so well under Judy's perceptive scrutiny.

"You're not at all like Elise Everett, in any case, full of her own self-importance. Or that other young actress he's ordered to be here," Judy continued, lowering her tone so only Morgana could hear her. "Both very talented on-screen, but shallow and useless off it. Expecting everyone to run around after them. But you're not like that, are you."

"Um, no," Morgana said, thinking of how hard she

worked every day running her own business. "But I've heard only nice things about Elise Everett and Georgiana Grace."

This wasn't quite true. Morwenna had said a lot of scathing things about both actresses, despite the fact she'd never met them. But Morgana had put it down to her sister's usual acid tongue and ignored most of it. Her impressions were, thus far, built only by what she'd read about them online before making the trip.

"Well, I'm not one to gossip," Judy's tone was conspiratorial and Morgana decided that Judy did in fact *love* to gossip. "But I know stories that would make your hair turn white. Georgiana is horrendously fake, it isn't even her real name. She pretends to be upper crust but she's not at all. She's actually called Georgia Spud, can you imagine?"

Morgana bit back her smile at the other woman's glee. "I can quite see why she changed it in that case," Morgana said, as diplomatically as she could. "And Elise?"

"She's awful, mean spirited, you know? She only holds on to her poor husband so no one else can have him. Someone's going to murder her one day, mark my words!"

Chapter Four

Morgana turned as she heard someone else enter the room, and found an elderly lady standing there. The newcomer was at least 80 and wore a high necked Victorian dress in violent purple. A matching feather boa fluttered around her neck, though it had clearly seen better days, and half the feathers were bent or broken.

"Grandmama," Lord Latheborne went forward to lead her into the room. "You've already met Bernie and Judy Gossard." He was obviously saying it to remind her. "But this glamorous young lady is Morwenna Emrys."

Morgana wasn't sure how he managed to get quite so much distaste into her introduction, but he did.

"Miss Emrys, this is The Dowager Baronness of Latheborne." He helped his grandmother lower herself down into a chair as he spoke.

Morgana instantly came forward and bent low, waiting until the hand was proffered before she extended her own to shake it, and also waiting for the other woman to speak first as her father had taught her many years ago.

"Just Baroness if you don't mind, at least until my grandson takes a wife." The elderly lady gave Morgana's hand a surprisingly hearty shake for someone who looked so frail. "Being called *The Dowager* makes me feel old."

"Pleased to make your acquaintance, Baroness," Morgana said, politely. "You have a lovely home."

"It's not really mine, despite the fact I've lived here sixty years," the lady replied acerbically, shooting her grandson a grumpy glare. "Did I hear Adams say sherry?"

As The Baroness had clearly lost interest in her, Morgana moved back to Judy. At that moment The Baroness barked an order at apparently empty air. "Leave the fire alone, it's clean enough!"

"Mad as a coot, poor dear," Judy whispered, looking delighted at the eccentricity.

Morgana nodded distractedly, but she was more surprised than anything. She knew perfectly well that The Baroness was looking directly at the ghost house-maid, and the ghost reacted at once, dropping a quick curtsey and scurrying from the room. Morgana's hand instinctively went to her crystal, and she felt momentarily off balance when it wasn't there, around her neck, where it usually hung. She moved her hand to her chest and calmed herself as she felt it's soothing vibrations coming from her bra.

"Curiouser and curiouser," she muttered.

"What?" Judy asked.

"Hmm?" Morgana looked at her, still distracted.

"You were quoting Alice in Wonderland, dear. Has something perplexed you?"

"No, no it's nothing." Morgana's eyes returned to the Baroness. Did she have some psychic ability? The lady could, obviously, see the ghost. Yet, she didn't seem to realise it *was* a ghost. It might even be the case that the ghost was trapped because the Baroness expected her to be there?

"Why are we sitting in here?" The Baroness complained loudly and suddenly. "Oliver?"

Lord Latheborne was by her side in an instant,

topping up her sherry glass himself. "Because we have guests, Grandmama. I did explain it to you."

"I don't like Americans," the Baroness stated, glaring at him. "Came to the war far too late, and they're always fat."

Judy stiffened beside her, and Morgana bit hard on her lip, trying not to laugh at the inappropriateness of it. Even without her senses open, she could tell that Judy was itching to respond in kind.

Lord Latheborne cast them an apologetic glance.

"We're lucky they came when they did," Bernie said with a droll laugh. "We could all be German now without their help, and this place wouldn't have survived it."

The Baroness gave a haughty sniff but said nothing more as she sipped her sherry and gazed into the fire.

"I'd put her in a nursing home if she was my grandmother," Judy muttered, still fixing the oblivious Baroness with a mean stare.

"I think she's marvellous, just for comedy value," Morgana replied cheerfully, and was greatly relieved when Judy's face relaxed into an appreciative smile.

"She is that," Judy agreed.

"I think this room would make a great setting for the proposal scene," Bernie waved his hand expansively at the surroundings. "Don't you Morwenna?"

Morgana choked briefly on her drink, unaware that she was supposed to have read the script. "Oh, ah, yes definitely," she said, desperately hoping he wouldn't want to talk details.

"Well, I think the rose garden is just darling," Judy put in. "Not in this weather, of course, but they'll be in bloom when you start filming, Bernie, and don't you think roses just shout romance?"

"Good point, you always know best." Bernie gave his wife an indulgent smile and Judy preened slightly.

"How about when the men are preparing to go pheasant shooting? That scene would work in here?" Judy glanced at the carpet beneath their feet and tapped her foot against it. "I don't suppose you know what's under this, do you, my lord?"

Lord Latheborne looked horrified. "No. And no one would get ready for a pheasant shoot in a drawing-room."

"That doesn't matter." Judy shook her head. "It's the appearance of grandeur that will appeal to the viewers."

"Now, now. We want authenticity with this one," Bernie admonished gently. "Not that I don't think you're right. Most of our audience would lap up the cornicing and such like. Genuine Victorian features are very popular."

"Georgian," Lord Latheborne corrected through gritted teeth. "This room is Georgian. The tower is Victorian if that helps, and the kitchens are the original Elizabethan part of the building. Latheborne Manor has been enhanced and added to a great deal over the centuries."

"Fascinating." Bernie looked entranced. "I must add all that into the script somehow. I can see we still have plenty to talk about."

"What about taking down that ancient portrait over the fireplace and replacing it with one of Dickie?" Judy suggested brightly. "He'd be thrilled to feature in the film as an ancestor, and probably double his financial input. We could get one painted especially, silly moustache and all."

Their eyes all turned to the picture that hung above the fire.

"That *ancient portrait* is my late husband," came the Baroness' voice from her chair. "He'd set the dogs on you."

Judy started, having forgotten that the old lady was listening. "Everything would be put back exactly as it is." she said, giving the old lady a patronising smile and managing not to sound remotely sorry.

Morgana realised she was actually enjoying herself at that moment. Particularly the clashes of culture, which she found more amusing than embarrassing. *Maybe it won't be so bad after all*, she thought, *especially with the Baroness here.*

At that moment the sound of a car pulling up was clearly heard, and a horn tooted twice.

Lord Latheborne tutted loudly, and Morgana gave him a questioning look.

"It's the signal for the butler to come and take in the bags. Except nobody has done that in this house for at least a hundred years," he told her in an undertone as they both moved toward the window.

"Is it considered *non-u* these days?" Morgana teased.

"Extremely," he agreed with feeling. He turned to his butler. "I suppose you'd better go and see to them, Adams. Sorry."

Morgana gave Lord Latheborne another speculative look. She hadn't known all that many peers in her life, but she thought it was probably rare that they apologised to their butlers for having to carry bags. If he didn't dislike her so much then she might have been rather impressed by him.

She looked with interest out of the window as several people emerged from the vehicle. The driver was first out, wearing a business suit and looking harried, he rushed around to open the door to the back of the car, at the same time as a woman let herself out of the passenger seat. She too wore a suit and grimaced as she tried to brush some of the wrinkles out of it before looking up at the house with admiration.

Morgana took in the woman, unsure if this was the film star, Elise Everett. She'd seen photos of Elise, and this woman definitely bore a striking resemblance to her. But her face was sweet and she wore very little makeup and her hair was more brown than Morgana had expected. She also looked anxious, which didn't fit at all with the image of a socialite that she'd been portrayed as.

From the back emerged another woman of similar age and appearance, but she was pristine. A jaunty hat perched on her waved golden locks, and she wore a fitted red dress in an exact matching shade to the hat. She waited, and a second later a red coat was passed out to her from a hand still inside the car. She swung it around her shoulders and walked toward the front door, ignoring her companions.

"Elise loves red," Judy commented, confirming Morgana's thoughts that she must be the second woman and not the first.

Morgana watched as a third, younger, woman followed her out of the car, this time wearing an old fashioned maid's outfit.

"Good grief," Morgana heard Lord Latheborne

mutter.

Bernie went out into the hall to greet the party as Adams opened the door. The rest of them looked with interest through the open doorway as Bernie opened his arms wide and gave Elise two kisses without actually touching her at all.

"Oh, this place is just perfect," Elise enthused, looking upward just as Morgana had. "Like stepping back in time, to an era before taste. I do hope they've modernised the bathrooms?"

"Of course," Bernie reassured her, "and you're very lucky that his Lordship's not married as it means you can have the whole Master Suite." He lowered his voice slightly to say, "But I didn't expect you to bring quite so many people with you, I thought it was just you and Harvey?"

"You can't possibly expect me to travel without Bonny? She has the most irritating foreign accent, but a lady needs her maid. And, as we are only in England for a short time, it made sense to combine my trip here with seeing my sister. You remember my sister Katherine, don't you?" She clicked her fingers toward her companions. "Kitty? Come and say hello to the greatest Director ever."

The woman in the crumpled suit stepped forward. "I'm really sorry about this, Bernie. I hope it won't put you out too much, but Elise insisted."

Bernie looked towards Lord Latheborne, who now followed him out into the hall. Lord Latheborne managed a tight smile and said, "I'm sure it can be accommodated. But I'm afraid not all the bedrooms have been refurbished yet, the blue room is mostly done, but the windows are a little drafty and the chimney makes a weird noise when it rains, which it will later."

"I'm sure it will be lovely," Kitty said, gratefully. "The windows in my flat in London don't even open, so a little draft will be a pleasant change."

Lord Latheborne gave her a warm smile that completely transformed his face, and shook her hand in welcome.

Elise looked slightly put out at having her sister greeted before her by the Lord of the Manor and put her hand on Kitty's arm in what looked to be a vice-like grip. Kitty winced and stepped to one side.

"I'm charmed to make your acquaintance, Lord Latheborne. Bernie has told me all about you and this house, though, why on earth you'd chose to live out here at the edge of civilisation..." Elise stopped as though words failed her.

"At your service, madam," he replied, through clenched teeth.

She either didn't notice or chose to ignore his irritation. "And this is my husband. Hurry up, darling, why must you make such a meal of everything? Let the servant do those bags on his own!"

The harried man, whom Morgana had taken to be a hired driver, dropped two suitcases at the foot of the stairs and came to her side.

Morgana felt a tug on her arm and turned to see Judy trying to pull her away from the door and back into the room.

"Another drink?" Judy said, stopping at the drinks trolley.

"Oh, not quite yet." Morgana looked down at her

own, which she'd barely even taken a sip of.

"You're going to need it," Judy warned. "But it should be entertaining. Guess why she's brought her sister?"

Morgana raised her brows questioningly.

"Because her sister is in love with Elise's husband, and him with her. Elise likes forcing them together and enjoys how much pain it brings them. It's her way of punishing them."

"But...if that's true, why do they let her?" Morgana was horrified that anyone would deliberately be that cruel.

"She doesn't really give them any choice. They can't admit how they feel, so they have to pretend it's fine."

"Why doesn't he leave her and marry the sister instead?" Morgana asked, checking over her shoulder that none of them had come into the room yet.

"I'm not sure, fear most likely," Judy looked frustrated by her lack of knowledge on the subject. "Or a prenup maybe? She controls the money."

"But if he loves Kitty then the money shouldn't matter," Morgana said.

"How refreshing that you believe that." Judy shook her head at Morgana in mock wonder. "Oh, look, snapping at Elise's heels as always." Judy pointed out the window to a sports car zooming up the drive. "Georgiana Grace is probably the biggest threat to Elise in Hollywood right now. Very similar style and look too. Both of them English by birth, and able to do perfect English and American accents, but Georgie is younger and hungrier. Too hungry for it, if you ask me!" Judy's face darkened unpleasantly for a moment, but then her vague and cheerful demeanour returned. "Just Dickie and Keefe still to come and the whole group will be here."

"You seem to know everyone quite well," Morgana observed.

"Indeed; my father was a director too, you know. Did a few of the Rat Pack movies, I remember Frank Sinatra putting me on his knee. It's my life, my blood. So, yes, they come and they go but I know them all."

"I bet you remember all their secrets too, don't you?" Morgana said, her eyes twinkling.

Judy threw back her head to laugh loudly. "Did I tell you yet that I like you?"

Morgana didn't have time to answer as at that moment everyone seemed to come through the door at once into the Drawing Room, all talking at the same time.

Lord Latheborne seemed much more impressed by Georgiana Grace than he was by either Morgana or Elise, as he went straight to the drinks trolley to pour her one and then another for Kitty as an afterthought. He ignored everybody else. In the absence of Adams the butler, it fell to Bernie to fetch drinks for Elise and her husband, Harvey. While this was going on Morgana took the opportunity to look over the latest newcomer.

Georgiana was stunning. Her hair was golden blonde, almost the exact same shade as Elise, but her dress and jacket were dusky pink, in contrast to Elise's more strident red.

Judy was right, Morgana thought. Georgiana was basically a younger version of Elise. The two women did look very similar. Both had the same peaches and cream complexion, and their clothes could have come from the same store.

The same designer, not store, Morgana reminded herself. Women like this didn't pop to Marks and Spencer for their power suits. She looked down at her own clothes. She'd chosen some of the most daring outfits from her wardrobe in an effort to emulate Morwenna's usual taste, but now she felt a bit wanton in her dress. It was knee-length and practical when teamed with her long brown boots, but the neckline did plunge rather low, and also left a great deal of her shoulders exposed. Perhaps she ought to have bought a 'travelling outfit' as these other women clearly had.

Then she reminded herself that her travel had barely consisted of going one county over, from Cornwall to the border of Devon, and she wasn't going to spend money buying new clothes just to fake being Morwenna for three days.

"You must be Morwenna," a voice said, breaking her out of her thoughts. "I'm Georgie, second fiddle to Elise's first fiddle." Georgiana stuck out her hand to Morgana who shook it in return.

"I guess that makes me third fiddle?" Morgana said with a smile.

"You can be second with me," Georgie replied. "At least you get to be one of the good guys. You're the best friend and confidant, right? I have to be the irritating interloper who tries to take her man."

Morgana looked confused.

"In the film," Georgie clarified. "You're set to play Elise's best friend, aren't you?"

"Oh." Morgana's face cleared. "Yes, of course."

"Seems such a faff, gathering us all here months before filming even starts. But Bernie was insistent that we get familiar with the house and each other. He likes to know everyone will get along and play well together, not that there is much hope of that. Mind you, I love our Lord and host, don't you? Isn't he just the dashing Darcy?" Georgie's eyes lingered on Lord Latheborne and Morgana had to admit to herself that she saw what the other girl meant.

"But this weather!" Georgie continued, looking toward the window, which was growing dark and misting up as a drizzle started outside. "Isn't it so dreary? I heard there's a storm coming, which means we're stuck inside together. At least in L.A. you can escape from your co-workers into the sunshine and there's a lot of fun things to do. Oh, wow!" Georgie broke off suddenly, her eyes widening as she stared toward the door.

A man stepped through it. His black hair glistening with droplets of rain, his broad shoulders shaking off a coat to reveal an immaculate suit, and his large eyes taking them all in.

"Keefe Mohan," Georgie and Morgana intoned almost simultaneously, both sounding reverential. They grinned at each other, recognizing the shared feeling. Morgana assumed most people felt like that when they first laid eyes on Keefe.

She knew who he was. Half the world probably did. He was definitely the most famous person in the room, and definitely the most handsome man that Morgana had ever seen in real life. She knew from magazines that his mother was Irish and his father was Indian, and the combination of their looks had made a man who could have been sculpted by Michelangelo. He'd been raised in Bangladesh, and then moved to America when he was eleven. The trace of his original accent only made him even more attractive.

Georgie went forward to introduce herself to Keefe Mohan, but Morgana held back. She felt like she almost faded into the curtains as she watched the vivacious Georgie and the equally vivacious Elise both circulating the room and talking loudly to everyone. She did notice, however, that apart from a perfunctory air kiss the first time they crossed paths, they then completely avoided each other.

Adams refilled her glass and Morgana found herself starting to get bored. Everyone was talking about themselves, but Morgana couldn't do that and she certainly didn't want to spend the evening talking about Morwenna. She managed to speak briefly to Keefe Mohan, but the entire conversation was like pulling teeth. He was polite, but he asked no questions and gave her very short answers to hers. She wondered if she just wasn't interesting enough to hold his attention.

"They're all rather intimidating, aren't they?" Elise's sister, Kitty, came to stand beside her.

"Certainly very confident. A lot of big personalities in one room," Morgana said. "I think my own personality is more *normal sized*, so it's hard to shine in this company."

"Me too," Kitty agreed. "Plus, nobody actually *wants* to talk to me. I'm just the mousy sister. The one who never achieved anything."

Morgana felt a pang of sympathy. Sometimes her own sister made her feel that way, but not to the point of damaging her own self-esteem. "What do you do, in your normal life?"

"I'm just a secretary. Elise once came to my office and found me spending an hour untangling a ball of paperclips. She thought it was hilarious and tells everyone about it whenever we're in the same room. Harvey is always kind to me though, he never asks me to file anything." Kitty gave an embarrassed laugh.

"Never underestimate the importance of a well organised file. My own books are a nightmare to keep straight." Morgana silently cursed herself. She was having trouble staying in character. Would she really be able to keep up the act for the entire weekend?

"Sherry." A bony finger poked Morgana hard in the backside. She jumped and looked down, realising she had placed herself next to the Baroness in an effort to get closer to the warmth of the fire.

"Yes, of course, Baroness," she looked over to the drinks and saw Adams in deep conversation with Keefe as he mixed the other man a cocktail. It would probably be easier to get it herself. "Sweet or dry?"

"Sweet." The old lady held out her empty glass and Morgana took it, and fetched the drink.

"The girl sweeping the fire, does she have a name?" Morgana asked, when she returned with the sherry.

The Baroness didn't answer immediately, she gave Morgana a beady-eyed look instead. Eventually, she said, "No-one has swept that fire in weeks, I'm just off my rocker."

"I don't believe that."

The old lady smiled. "I prefer the past to the future. The past never changes, you see? Good or bad, you can not affect it. My grandson, he's always looking forwards. Progression, he calls it. Putting in modern conveniences. And now, this revolting lot, tramping all over the house. Have you any idea the damage those high heels do to wooden floors?"

"I'm sure Lord Latheborne has the best interests of the house at heart." Morgana pulled an upright chair from the wall and sat down beside the Baroness.

"He does," the lady said, grudgingly. "He's a good boy, seven years in the Navy took the wildness out of him. He was ever such a wild child, practically feral. Running all over the estate with only the dogs for company, keeping mice in his pocket, and sleeping in a treehouse."

"Seems a pity he had to grow up." Morgana looked over to Lord Latheborne who had been studiously ignoring her for most of the time so far, and thought to herself that they'd probably have gotten along famously as children. "I think he's too uptight now, a night in a treehouse might be just the thing to remind him who he was."

The baroness stared into the fire, which was throwing off heat and light now that the ghost housemaid had been scared away. "He has a lot of responsibilities, this house is a burden. Needs a woman in it with some sense of style." Her eyes raked over Morgana. "Are you single?"

Morgana laughed loudly, drawing eyes to her. She lowered her voice to reply. "I'm flattered, but I don't think you'd like my style, it's more earthy than classy."

"You'll do," the Baroness said, firmly.

Morgana decided that it wasn't worth arguing the

point. "Will you excuse me?" She rose to her feet and looked out the window. The sky outside was pitch black now and the rain came down with a vengeance, beating against the glass panes. Morgana took the opportunity to sidle up to Bernie.

"Is the man that I'm supposed to be charming to still coming?"

She'd already decided that Morwenna wouldn't be coy about it, and was doing her best to act just like her sister, but perhaps with a slightly less acerbic tongue.

Bernie looked at his watch. "He should be here already. I can't get any cell reception in this damn house, though, so I don't know if he's running late. Perhaps we should give up for now and go and change for dinner."

Morgana groaned silently to herself. She hadn't really anticipated having to change for dinner and she wasn't sure her limited wardrobe was going to stand the pressure if it was a different outfit for every meal.

"Okay folks," Bernie declared loudly to the room. "It's already six-thirty, so we're not going to wait for Dickie any longer. I suggest we retire to our rooms and reconvene in about half an hour for dinner?"

There were murmurs of assent, and Morgana was sure that she wasn't the only one feeling the effects of drinking on an empty stomach. She'd just reached the door back to the hall when there was a bang and all the lights went out.

Chapter Five

"Keep calm, everyone. It's probably just a fuse." Lord Latheborne's voice rang out over the sudden hubbub of distressed sounds from the female guests.

There was a flare as a match was struck and she could see the outline of a man in the glow of the fire as he lit the candles on the mantelpiece. Adams came hurrying in, also carrying a candle, and they were all soon bathed in a warm flickering light as more candles were distributed around the room.

"How on earth are we supposed to get ready in the dark? There must be a generator or something?" Bernie could be seen glaring at his host.

"A generator?" Lord Latheborne looked amused. "This is Devon, not the Antarctic. It's just the storm, it won't last long."

"But no electricity means no hot water," Georgie wailed.

"That's not acceptable! Fix it at once," Elise demanded.

Morgana thought she saw Lord Latheborne roll his eyes in the light of the flickering flame, but his voice was friendly as he said, "The hot water is gas, not electricity." Picking up a candlestick, he left the room with it.

"I'm used to this, it'll be off for hours." The dark shape of the Baroness rose from her chair. "I'm going to retire. Adams, have a tray sent to my room please?" She took a candle off the table and tottered out the door with it, quickly disappearing into the darkness beyond.

"Oh well, what better excuse for another drink," Judy commented, moving up beside Morgana.

They spoke in hushed voices for a while, and Morgana wondered if they felt as she did, that the house suddenly seemed very large and foreboding in the dark. Of course, it didn't help that she could see the ghost that came and went now that Baroness had gone, even if the others were oblivious to it.

Ten minutes later Lord Latheborne was back, his mouth set in a grim line. "It's not a fuse, it's the storm," he said, shrugging as a couple of groans came from the people who knew what that meant. "We're not going to have any power for a while, possibly until morning," he continued. "So, can I suggest that we eat now, as dinner is ready anyway, and then call it a night?"

Elise began complaining about 'being forced to stay in a backwater' until her husband put an arm around her. "It will be an adventure, Lissy. Dinner by candlelight."

"Oh please," she scoffed in reply. "Let's just get through it and then I'm taking a pill. Hopefully, it will all be over by the time I wake up, if not then we're leaving at first light!"

"I bet his Lordship is thinking of keeping the electricity off on purpose now," Judy whispered to Morgana as they crossed the hall to the dining room. "It's the obvious way to get rid of us all quickly."

Morgana had to agree. She'd be distinctly tempted to do the same herself.

The dining room, however, was a very welcome sight. Adams brought all the candles through from the drawing-room and soon it looked quite cheerful and romantic as they sat around the table.

"What about Bonny?" Kitty suddenly said, as she watched Lord Latheborne's maid, Louise, bring in a huge tureen of soup. "She must be sitting in her room all alone in the dark!"

"No, miss," Louise said, shaking her head. "Bonny is in the kitchen, we've a kerosene lamp in there, and all the hobs lit. It's light enough."

"That's a relief, isn't it, Elise?" Kitty looked at her sister, who lifted one shoulder in an uncaring gesture.

Morgana saw Kitty and Elise's husband, Harvey, exchange a look. Judy had been right about the two of them; they shared a common bond of some sort, even it was just that they both acknowledged Elise's shortcomings.

Morgana found herself seated between Harvey and an empty chair. Lord Latheborne took the head of the table, with Georgiana on one side of him and Judy on the other. Bernie Gossard sat at the other end, with Elise next to him and Kitty on his other side. Keefe Mohan was between Judy and Elise, who both looked very pleased. Morgana noticed, though, that he didn't really engage them in conversation, merely giving them polite replies to their enquiries.

After the soup, which was very good and warming, they were served chicken in a white wine and tarragon sauce, with leek and potatoes. Morgana watched as the other women scraped the sauce off their chicken and left all of their potatoes. She chuckled to herself that she didn't have to care about such things, and was extremely thankful that she was only playing the part of someone who might worry, rather than actually needing to.

She saw Lord Latheborne watching her curiously as she tucked greedily into the excellent food, and she cocked an eyebrow at him in challenge.

He smiled, his eyes holding hers, and there was a new warmth there that made Morgana immediately flush and look away. She kept her gaze fixed to her plate for a moment as she tried to get a handle on which emotion she was suddenly feeling.

Attraction?

That would be inconvenient, she decided. She could hardly entertain any kind of flirtation when she was pretending to be Morwenna! But he definitely had a certain charisma about him. A strong life force. She focussed instead on Keefe, who was sitting opposite her.

"Is this your first time in Devon?" she asked.

He nodded. "I come to England occasionally for filming, but mostly just stay in London. I did visit Sherwood once, I'm a fan of Robin Hood."

"Really?" Morgana looked at him in surprise. "Do you mean the Robin Hood movies or the actual legends?"

"Both. I very much like the idea of the man who fought back against the injustices of the time. He represented an ideal. It's a rare quality. I also envy him the anonymity his disguise gave him."

"And the fantastic legs he had in those tights," Georgie chimed in.

"That too," Keefe's mouth tilted up at one corner. "But this part of Devon is very desolate in comparison, too exposed."

"People find beauty in that," Morgana said. "The wind sculpts the rocks around here into shapes that seem mythical, and there are stone circles out on the moor that date back about four thousand years. It's worth checking out."

Morgana was aware of Lord Latheborne still watching her with curiosity, but she forced herself not to glance at him.

"Perhaps tomorrow you could show me some of these stone circles?" Keefe replied, finally looking interested in something.

"We can all go," Georgiana said, enthusiastically.

"Tomorrow will be taken up with touring the house," Bernie's voice was reprimanding. "This is a work weekend. We need to familiarise ourselves with the rooms we'll be using for filming. You all need to look at home here, and with each other too. It's my method and it works."

The interest in Keefe's eyes died and his attention drifted away as he watched the butler clear their plates. Morgana chewed her lip and wondered whether to try again with a new topic, then decided she couldn't be bothered. Keefe Mohan was beautiful to look at, but difficult to talk to.

Georgiana leaned across the empty chair to speak in a lowered voice. "Bernie always does this. He gathers his lead characters on location and then gets in a total huff when we don't instantly bond. He says it shows in the film."

"He's probably right though," Morgana said, thoughtfully. She'd not really considered it before, but surely on-screen chemistry had to come from somewhere? Or were they all too good as actors to need it to be real?

Georgiana nodded discreetly toward Elise. "You think so?"

Morgana knew exactly what she meant. It would be

hard for anyone to bond with Elise. Humour danced in Georgiana's eyes as she saw that Morgana had picked up on her point.

"Just how local are you?" Lord Latheborne asked Morgana, surprising her with his direct question.

"Portmage," she answered, delighted that he seemed to have dropped his disapproval toward her. "North coast of Cornwall, just over the border."

"That's closer than I'd imagined. I had you pegged as a city girl." He sipped at his wine, looking at her speculatively over the brim.

Morgana felt a desire to be honest with him, but she had to stay true to her role. "Born and raised in the village, though I live in London for now."

"It seems as though Hollywood has come knocking at your door, will you move to America now as your colleagues have all done?" He narrowed his eyes, as though testing her somehow.

"I still keep a house in London," Georgiana put in, almost indignantly, and Morgana was glad to be spared answering with any kind of a lie.

There was a pause in the conversation as dessert was set down. Adams and Louise bustled about the table, giving everyone a slice of chocolate torte.

"Is there any chance of having fruit salad instead?" Elise queried down the table to Lord Latheborne.

"No," Louise answered, banging down the plate in front of Elise.

Morgana bit her lip to avoid laughing as she watched Lord Latheborne smother his own chuckle as a cough. He tried to look apologetic when Elise pouted at him, fury showing in the tightening of her lips, but he didn't manage to pull it off.

"Then I suppose we shall have to go to bed." Elise began to rise to her feet, but a sudden bang from the front hall made them all turn to look at the door.

"Uncle Oliver?" A voice called out. "Where the bloody hell is everyone? Hullo? Are we having a power cut or have you all buggered off out?"

The voice was cultured and immediately portrayed a young man with a very expensive British education.

Lord Latheborne let out a groan and then raised his voice. "We're in the dining room, Ethan."

Ethan Cope bounded into the room energetically, unwinding a scarf from around his neck and handing it along with his coat to Adams, at the same time as clapping the butler hard on the shoulder in greeting.

Elise, still on her feet, stretched out a hand toward the newcomer but he ignored it, his attention still on the butler.

"Adams! You're still putting up with the old man then? I swear you get more handsome every time I see you."

Even in the candlelight, it was impossible to miss Adams turning bright red with pleasure at these words.

"I'm hardly old," Lord Latheborne said grumpily, not moving from his chair as he glared at his nephew. "And don't flirt with Adams, I can't afford to lose him. What are you doing here, Ethan?"

"The rumour on the grapevine is that you're hosting a house party and I had to come and see it for myself. Plus, I heard Morwenna would be here." Ethan's gaze swept the table, coming to rest on Morgana. He gave her a slow and lingering sultry smile.

Morgana shifted in her chair and gave him an uncomfortable half-smile in return.

Damn you, Morwenna, she thought. *How on earth do I handle this?*

"Ethan," Elise made an effort to capture his attention. "I'm so delighted to finally meet you. We have so many friends in common, and I genuinely admired your Darwin." She proffered her hand again, this time practically waving it in his face.

Ethan looked at her blankly for a moment, then clasped the hand and bowed over it in a charming fashion. "Elise Everett, my apologies, I didn't immediately recognise you in the dim light in here. It's a pleasure."

Morgana heard Lord Latheborne smother another laugh at his nephew's hasty gallantry.

"As you're here, I suppose you'd better join us." Lord Latheborne stood and quickly made the rest of the introductions. "Elise, you've just met, and this is her sister, Katherine, and her husband, Harvey Everett. Bernie you know, of course, and have you met Judy Gossard, his wife? This radiant vision on my right is Georgiana Grace, I'm sure Keefe Mohan needs no introduction." He looked at Morgana and his expression darkened. "And you're apparently already old friends with Morwenna Emrys."

Ethan nodded to everyone, giving only Bernie a handshake before moving round the table to the empty chair between Morgana and Georgiana. "Is this seat free? How perfect."

"We were expecting Dickie Magnus, but it rather looks as though he won't be appearing tonight," Bernie said, looking a trifle put out. "Still," he added cheerfully, "you're a welcome edition, Ethan. Maybe I can persuade you to do a cameo in the movie?"

"Maybe. I'm not all that difficult to persuade," Ethan replied smoothly, staring straight into Morgana's eyes as he said it. He reached out to take her hand that was resting on the table, but Morgana snatched it away before he made contact.

The boy now sitting beside her was certainly good looking, but young, and she wasn't very impressed with the larger than life confidence that he was throwing around.

Elise looked extremely put out as she watched Ethan bestow all his attention on Morgana. "I'm going to bed. Come along, Harvey, and you too, Kitty, you look dreadfully haggard and I'm sure you could use a good night's sleep."

Kitty dropped the fork she'd been using to eat her dessert and looked hurt. Harvey gave her an apologetic grimace, but they both rose to their feet.

"Better each take a candle," Lord Latheborne said, with a hint of devilry in his tone. "There are ghosts in this house and things tend to happen in the dark."

Elise gave a horrified gasp at his words and looked around her as though a ghost were about to attack at any moment.

"That wasn't very kind, my Lord," Judy admonished him lightly.

"No. My apologies," he said, not looking remotely sorry.

"Have Bonny sent up to my room," Elise said, haughtily and swept out, followed by her husband and her sister.

"She doesn't even remember that we've met before," Ethan commented quietly to Morgana. "She wasn't remotely interested in me when I was a nobody, but now I'm well-known she acts as though we should be friends."

"She did a slander piece on me when I first started getting known," Georgiana said, moving her chair a little closer. "It nearly destroyed my career before I'd even got going. If Bernie hadn't taken me under his wing then I doubt I'd have continued."

Morgana furrowed her brow. "Can't you sue for something like that?"

"I couldn't afford to take her on at the time, and most people have forgotten it now, so I don't want to drag it all up." Georgiana shrugged her shoulders. "Everyone knows she's a nightmare to work with, but she's a big name, and movies need that to succeed."

"Well, I think you're much prettier than she is, and I've no doubt you'll be even bigger soon," Ethan said to Georgiana, making her blush.

"I think I'll retire too," Morgana said, refusing a coffee and deciding to make her escape while Ethan's attention was focussed on Georgiana.

"Us too," Judy put down her napkin. "Bernie?"

"Yes, my dear, I'll be up later. Might just have a glass of port with his Lordship."

Judy looked disapproving but didn't say anything more.

Morgana smiled at Adams as he cleared her dessert plate. "Please tell the housekeeper that dinner was fantastic."

"Mrs. Brown will be pleased," Adams nodded.

"Goodnight, everyone. See you in the morning." Morgana picked up a candle and followed Judy out of the room, glad of the company as they ascended the wide creaking stairs. The wind howled from somewhere in the house, and thunder rolled in the distance.

Morgana felt a shiver of apprehension. She'd loved storms as a child, been exhilarated by them. But since the death of her father at sea, she heard thunder now more as a portent of doom.

Chapter Six

Morgana surveyed her bedroom. It was a softly feminine room, with yellow walls, a pale blue bedspread, and matching curtains. Her suitcase was beside her bed, and she hurried over to it, extracting her phone.

She felt unsettled being somewhere new, and particularly so as everyone around her was a complete stranger. Worse, she felt like a fraud. She was completely out of her depth with their film talk, and she really didn't think she was going to be able to continue pretending to be Morwenna now that Ethan Cope was here. It had sounded as though he and Morwenna had been on intimate terms, which meant he was very likely to say or do something that put Morgana in a position of having to tell him the truth.

She cursed when her mobile phone failed to find any reception. No internet either. She badly wanted to call her sister and get some reassurance, or maybe just yell at her, she hadn't decided which yet.

It will all be easier in the morning, she decided. *I'll avoid Ethan and stick with Judy and Georgiana.* She also wanted to avoid Bernie as much as possible as he knew Morwenna too, and she had no desire to be around Elise. Lord Latheborne was another she needed to keep her distance from. Being attracted to him was extremely inconvenient, especially as he thought she'd had a relationship with his nephew and because he seemed to dislike her.

She glanced at her watch and groaned when she realised it was only nine pm. She wasn't remotely tired.

Knowing that she needed to ground herself,

Morgana went back into her suitcase and pulled out her tarot cards. She settled on the window seat and looked out into the rainy night.

She separated out the minor arcana, wanting a quick and basic reading, and put them to one side. Then she shuffled the cards slowly, focussing on her need to feel calm and asking the ether whether she should stay.

She dealt three cards in a row, then one above the central card and one below it, and finally one sideways over the middle.

The initial spread told her where she was coming from, where she was now, where she was going. The card below was influences she brought with her, the one above was influences coming, the sideways card crossed her current position.

She looked at them for a long time, trying to divine meanings in the pattern and how they each connected.

"*Temperance*," she muttered. "Obviously me, before I came to this place. Why am I *The Priestess* now? How am I supposed to control things? Especially as I'm not even being myself. Maybe I need to exert my wisdom, keep things mellow?" That puzzled her, but not unduly.

She looked at the third card and chewed her lip. The Tower. "Something is going to happen, something I won't like. Great." She glared at the card.

The one below was The Hermit. "Hmm, that's not unexpected either. I'm hiding my true self. I just hope it's not more than that. I guess I have been living a bit of a quiet life recently, but I don't think I'm ready for any changes." She focussed on the card above the centre. "*The Moon*, that's not great either. Probably indicates my deception having consequences. Or could it be the deception of others? This lot definitely have skeletons in their closets."

But it was the card that crossed her that she spent the most time looking at. *"The Wheel of Fortune.* How does that apply? Things could go either way? Or both good and bad will happen?"

The minutes ticked by as she contemplated the cards and tried to make a decision. She was tempted to pack up at first light and call the whole thing off. Her senses were telling her that she should leave for some reason. But she'd made a commitment to Morwenna, and as annoying as her sister was, she had asked for a favour and Morgana had agreed to do it. Perhaps tomorrow the backer that she was supposed to be charming to would arrive and she could do her duty before she escaped the manor and got back to her real life.

She sighed, knowing that she wouldn't leave, not yet anyway, when a tapping came at her bedroom door.

Chapter Seven

Morgana looked at her watch, surprised to find an hour had passed. She took her time going to the door. She rather suspected that she was going to find Ethan Cope there and that she'd have to be quite firm with him to make him go away.

It came as a surprise to find Georgiana hovering, already in a silky nightdress, looking up and down the corridor as though in the act of doing something wicked.

Georgiana didn't wait to be invited in, she just rushed past Morgana and shut the door. "It's like Piccadilly Circus out there, you wouldn't believe all the people sneaking about."

Morgana grinned. "Including you. There was me thinking I was about to get lucky."

Georgie laughed. "Maybe you are?" Then she shook her head. "I was going somewhere else, but you never heard me say that. Unfortunately, I nearly got caught, so I thought you wouldn't mind if I ducked in here instead?"

"Not at all. I was pretty bored, to be honest. I can't get any phone signal, and I forgot to pack any books." Morgana gestured to the chair in front of her dressing table and plonked herself down on the bed.

"There's a library downstairs if you really want a book," Georgiana said, checking her reflection in the dressing table mirror. "Latheborne, Bernie, and Ethan went there for after-dinner port."

"No sign of Dickie Magnus then?"

"Didn't you hear? He's not coming after all, he left a message on Bernie's cell phone. Bernie was able to pick it up by going practically all the way to the roof. Funny thing though, Dickie says he's stuck in L.A. and can't get to England, but he isn't."

"Isn't what?" Morgana asked, confused.

"He isn't stuck in L.A. He was on the same plane as me. I saw him getting off when we landed, but then I lost him. I sailed out with my British passport, and he got caught in the crowd going through immigration." Georgiana frowned thoughtfully.

"That's certainly odd that he lied." Morgana shrugged. "But maybe he got a better offer? Some redhead on the plane perhaps." They shared a smile over that. "So, you decided not to go for drinks in the library? What about Keefe Mohan?"

"Keefe went up to bed after you. I was tempted to go to the library, just to put a kink in their boys-only session. But I've been up since five, I only flew in to London this morning. I was longing for a hot bath. Do you know that we're sharing a bathroom? And I think Kitty is lumped in with us too?" Georgiana pulled a face.

Morgana gave a look of mock horror in return. "Sharing a bathroom, in this day and age. Good grief, Georgiana, how will we manage?"

Georgiana held up her hands in humorous surrender. "I know, I know. I've become spoilt. Going from one hotel to another for years, it's made me forget how real people live. And you must call me Georgie, all my friends do."

"If we're friends then you have to tell me where you were sneaking off to? You looked like you were hitting it off with Ethan?" Morgana inquired, knowing she was being nosy.

"Oh please, he's much too young! I prefer older men."

"He's not that young, only, what, twenty-one, twenty-two?" Morgana guessed.

"And I'm thirty-eight, but you're not allowed to tell anyone that either!" Georgie confided.

"No way." Morgana was genuinely surprised. "I thought you were younger than me! You only look about twenty-five."

"Marry me," Georgie joked in response. "No, I'm ancient, but that's Hollywood for you. We all hold back the years as much as we possibly can. Did you know that Elise is actually forty? It's so dumb that she's going to play a woman half her real age."

Morgana's eyes widened again. "Really? That does seem unfair on younger actresses, does nobody get to play someone who is actually their own age?"

"Do *you*?" Georgie raised her brows at Morgana, and she remembered just in time that she was supposed to be more knowledgeable about this world than she sounded.

But Georgie's attention was now on the window. "Are those tarot cards?" She went over to have a look, and Morgana scrambled after her, feeling exposed by what the cards revealed.

"Yes, it's silly really. I just do a reading for myself when I'm feeling unsure."

"How enthralling! Will you do one for me?"

"Oh, um, I could I suppose."

"Don't worry, not tonight. I have a date to keep. Miss Grace, in the dining room, with the garter belt." Georgie gave her another wicked look and then stuck her head out the bedroom door. "It looks all clear. Now, remember, you didn't see me!"

Morgana went to the bathroom and took off her makeup and brushed her teeth, thinking about whether she should stay or go. If what Georgie had said about Dickie not coming anymore, then maybe she had a good excuse to leave early? Bernie had only really wanted Morwenna there to charm Dickie, she didn't need to be a part of the 'bonding' party. Morwenna's role in the movie was clearly not a large one, so maybe she would be able to go without compromising her promise to her sister?

She walked back down the hall, sighing with resignation as she saw Ethan leaning against the wall beside her bedroom door.

"There you are," he said, straightening as he caught sight of her.

"Ethan, listen. Whatever might have happened between us in the past..." She was cut off as Lord Latheborne appeared at the top of the stairs and made an interrupting noise with his throat. Both Morgana and Ethan turned their heads towards him.

"Not tonight, Ethan. Go to your room." Lord Latheborne said firmly, not even looking at Morgana.

"I'm a grown man, you can't seriously be saying that to me?" Ethan stared disbelievingly at his uncle. Morgana didn't know whether to be indignant or whether to laugh. Lord Latheborne was certainly making her feel like a naughty child, but at the same time, the look on Ethan Cope's face was priceless.

"Not with the Baroness in the house," Lord Latheborne bit out, his voice making it clear there was no room for argument.

Ethan scowled but didn't say another word. Instead, he stormed off down the corridor and round the corner. The sound of a door slamming came a moment later.

Morgana folded her arms defensively as she appraised Lord Latheborne. "Aren't you going to tell me to go to my room too? Or do I get a spanking first?"

For a moment she thought he was going to laugh, but then he sighed as though she was a great trial to him. "Just go to bed, Miss Emrys."

"What if I don't want to?" Some inner demon pushed her to say.

"While I'm sure there are any number of men here that might interest you, and vice versa, I'd prefer you not follow Ethan. Can you respect my wishes?" He asked so nicely that she was thrown slightly.

"I was about to send him packing, but you didn't even give me the chance!"

"Why don't I believe you?" His mouth kicked up at one corner, but she wasn't sure if was genuine humour or if he was mocking her.

"Because you've been down on me since I arrived?" Morgana suggested. "Because, maybe, you don't think I'm good enough for him?"

"If I've given you that impression then I apologise."

Morgana spread her hands in a gesture of defeat. Whatever his problem was, she couldn't argue with his manners. "I accept your apology, good night, my lord." She pushed open her bedroom door.

"Sleep well, Morwenna." He said it so softly that she turned back in surprise, but he'd vanished into the darkness.

Morgana lay in bed and thought about the people in

the house. The temptation was there to open her psychic senses and get a really good look at them, but it wasn't worth it. She'd just end up drained by it. There were too many big personalities in a small space. The best thing to do was to leave, the sooner the better.

She liked Bernie and Judy, but she didn't really trust either of them. Georgie was fun, but also definitely hiding something. Keefe Mohan was famous enough to be interesting, and she knew he was an amazing actor, but in person, he'd definitely been lacking. She wanted nothing to do with Elise and her entourage, she'd been able to feel the negativity around them even without her senses open. Which just left the enigmatic Lord Latheborne and the unwanted attention from Ethan Cope.

She made up her mind that she'd make her excuses and pack first thing in the morning, and tried to go to sleep. But sleep wouldn't come. She lay awake and wondered who Georgie was going to meet.

Keefe maybe? Then again, she'd been talking a lot at dinner with Lord Latheborne. Morgana felt irritated by that idea, perhaps because Lord Latheborne didn't seem to like her but he did like Georgie?

She tossed and turned for what felt like hours, and spent a great deal of the night wondering whether to sneak down to the library and find a book. But she didn't want to bump into anyone on the way. She felt as though she'd only just closed her eyes when a scream rang out and kept screaming.

Chapter Eight

Morgana sat up with a jerk and listened to the sudden banging of doors in the corridor outside her room. Without thinking she reached out to turn on her bedside lamp and then was startled when it worked.

"Electricity's back on, then." She looked at her watch, it was just gone five-thirty. She flopped back on her pillow. "If all this is because Elise has seen a spider, then I'm definitely going home," she grumbled.

But now she could hear male voices calling out, and someone was sobbing. She threw back the covers and look down at her red and blue check flannel pyjamas. They weren't a patch on Georgie's slinky satin nightdress, but at least she could be seen in them without feeling too exposed.

Out in the hall, she discovered Lord Latheborne blocking the door to a bedroom, Harvey Everett trying to push past him, and Kitty sitting on the floor, crying. Judy was wrapping a blanket around Bonny the maid, who was white and shaking, and as she watched in confusion, Bernie came out of the room that Lord Latheborne was guarding.

"What's going on?" Ethan said, appearing beside Morgana, tying the cord of his dressing gown and yawning. "It's still stupid o'clock, why is everyone up?"

Ethan's hair was a mess, but he still looked gorgeous. *Oh to be young and not even need to try to look that good*, Morgana thought enviously. She attempted to smooth down her own bedhead and wished she'd stopped to check her face.

"No idea," Morgana said, "but I think something has

happened." Her mind flashed back to the tarot cards she'd read the night before, specifically the card depicting a tower being struck by lightning.

A minute later Georgie also appeared, looking distinctly the worse for wear. "For God's sake, what's all the racket about?" she grumbled.

Bernie held out his hands to quiet them all down. "Can I suggest we all go down to the dining room and I'll tell you what's happened."

They all exchanged anxious looks and began to traipse to the stairs. "Where's Keefe?" Bernie asked, ushering them past him.

"Keefe takes sleeping pills," Georgie supplied. "He's probably not even aware anything's going on."

Morgana gave Georgie a side glance, deciding it now seemed likely that Keefe was the man she had been visiting the night before. Morgana stopped when she reached Kitty. "Can you stand?" she asked rubbing the back of the sobbing girl. "Come on, you don't want to stay here in this draughty corridor. Come downstairs, I'm sure we can sort out some coffee."

Kitty stood up, but she kept her hands to her face and continued to cry as Morgana steered her to the stairway.

As Ethan passed Lord Latheborne, his uncle's hand reached out to grab him by the elbow. Morgana was close enough to hear him speaking in a low voice.

"Go into my study and use the telephone there. Call the police and tell them there's been a murder, then find Mrs. Brown and ask her to bring me the spare key to this room."

Ethan nodded, and at the bottom of the stairs, he

went the opposite way to Morgana, who followed the others into the dining room.

Bernie came down last, escorting Harvey who was angry and didn't seem to want to move.

Judy insisted on taking Bonny into the kitchen. "The girl needs a calming cup of tea, with perhaps a spot of brandy in it," she declared.

"Don't we all," Georgie whispered to Morgana as they took the same seats they'd sat in the night before.

There was a pause as Bernie persuaded Harvey to sit down.

"I don't see why I should be kept out," Harvey fretted. "It's my room and my wife."

Keefe came in at this point. He'd dressed, but he looked older in the pale light of the sunrise, and not nearly so glamorous.

Morgana looked around and realised that all of them looked a lot less intimidating and perfect after being rudely awoken. She suddenly felt more comfortable and less like the country cousin.

"Right," Bernie said, as Harvey was finally quelled into silence. "I'm afraid I have some terrible news. There's no use beating about the bush, Elise Everett has just been discovered dead."

"Dead?" Georgie sounded stunned.

"To be precise, murdered. At some point in the night, she was stabbed. I'm sure the police will be able to determine when, but in the meantime, I think we should all wait in here together."

Morgana cleared her throat. "The assumption being that it was one of us?"

Everyone looked at Harvey and then quickly looked

away again.

"Or one of the staff?" Georgie suggested, hesitantly.

"Highly unlikely," Lord Latheborne said, coming through the door, with Ethan behind him. "Speaking of which, where on earth is Adams? He's usually the first up. I'd be amazed if he slept through all that hubbub."

"Here, Sir. My apologies, I didn't wish to appear undressed." Adams came through the door at the back of the room that Morgana assumed must lead to the kitchen. Adams was straightening his tie, and she noticed that he didn't have any socks on beneath his shoes, but he was otherwise the now the epitome of a perfect butler.

Judy followed him through the door. "I've settled Bonny in the kitchen, and Mrs. Brown is just starting to make the breakfasts."

"Can't we at least shower before breakfast?" Georgie complained.

"I don't think we should." Bernie frowned over this. "What if someone is washing away evidence? Blood on their hands and all that? I'm sure the police would rather we just waited here."

"I'm not being interviewed without a shower first," Keefe said, decisively. "You can not stop me from washing myself."

Morgana's mind turned to her previous dealings with the police. What if Detective Sergeant Tristan Treharne was on the job? Were they out of his area? She'd had a crush on him since girl-hood, and while she knew it could never happen, due to his dating her sister in their teens, she still wanted to look her best in front of him.

"I agree," she said, after some thought. "I want a

shower too."

There was some argument, but Morgana and several others got their way and were soon heading back upstairs. Morgana was extremely peeved when Georgie beat her to the bathroom, especially as Georgie had enjoyed the luxury of a bath the night before, but she supposed that if she'd spent the night with a man then she might be just as eager to freshen up.

An hour later, she was ready for breakfast. She'd chosen not to dress up like Morwenna this time. She needed to feel more like herself. So, she'd put on a thick jumper in emerald green to emphasise the new red streaks in her hair, and paired it with black jeans and ankle boots. The heel on the boots was much higher than she'd normally wear to work in her shop, but she had a weakness for boots and was pleased to find an occasion to wear this particular pair.

The first person she ran into when she left her room was Police Constable Poppy Dunn. She and another officer were moving about the bedroom of Elise Everett, and Morgana presumed they were processing the crime scene. She glimpsed the bed and saw that it was covered in blood.

"Hi, Morwenna," Poppy greeted her cheerfully as she went by. "Gosh, I can't get over how identical you and Morgana still look even after all these years."

Poppy had been in the same class at school with Morgana and Morwenna, and had been good friends with both.

"Then how do you know I'm Morwenna?" Morgana asked curiously.

"We were given a list of everyone who's here. Is it

true that Keefe Mohan is downstairs?" Poppy self-consciously tucked some hair behind an ear.

Morgana nodded, "And Ethan Cope." She grinned, well aware that her friend would fall over herself for a hot man, or a hot woman come to that.

"Oh geez." Poppy stopped what she was doing to move over to the mirror inside the bedroom. "Mind you, it's Keefe I most want to meet. That effeminate beauty on a man, it's almost too much to take."

"He's actually kind of dull in person," Morgana confided. "So, I assume you being here means Latheborne Manor falls under your area?"

"Yeah." Poppy continued to tidy her appearance in front of the mirror. "The DI and DS are downstairs, you'd probably better scoot."

Movement came from deeper inside the room, and a man that Morgana recognised as PC Cartwright stepped into view. "And you'd probably better get on with your job, Constable," he said grumpily. "I'm not doing all this by myself!"

Poppy gave Morgana an apologetic look and turned away from the mirror reluctantly, before pushing closed the bedroom door, so Morgana couldn't see anything more.

She went down the stairs slowly, trying to work out what to say to the Detective Inspector about who she really was. She didn't want to blow her cover and ruin things for Morwenna, but this wasn't really the time for subterfuge and they could both get into a lot of trouble if she lied about her identity during a murder investigation.

She went first to the dining room and was disappointed but unsurprised to find she'd missed breakfast and the room was empty. She stood and pondered whether to knock on the door to the kitchen, to see if there was any chance of getting some coffee, when a middle-aged woman backed through it, pulling a tea trolley.

"They're all in the large drawing-room, my duck," the woman said, stopping to rub her back. Morgana realised this must be the Housekeeper.

"Thank you, is that coffee?" She couldn't help inhaling deeply as she spotted the cafetierre on the trolley.

"Coffee, tea, and a good selection of biscuits," the Housekeeper confirmed. Her voice turned sympathetic. "Did you miss breakfast? I'm ever so sorry I couldn't keep it out longer, but with the police turning up…"

"Battle for the bathroom. I lost," Morgana explained, holding the door wide for the woman to pass through into the hall.

"Not surprising with them acting folks, God forbid they should be seen without their make up," the older woman chuckled. "At least with them all being on diets, you can tuck into the custard creams, should keep you going until lunch. Would you like me to sneak out some cake? I 'ave a lovely Battenberg in the fridge."

"That's really kind, but I'll be okay with the biscuits. Thanks." She was hungry, but she also didn't want Detective Sergeant Tristan Treharne to see her stuffing her face with cake. *I guess that makes me just as vain as the rest of them*, she thought ruefully.

She was disappointed, however, to reach the drawing-room and discover that neither Detective Inspector Lowen, or Tristan where anywhere to be seen.

Instead, she was greeted by a smaller group. Georgie, Ethan, Judy, Keefe, and Lord Latheborne were the only ones present. They all fell on the tea trolley and Morgana had to move fast to swipe the coffee pot before anyone else got to it.

"Where are the others?" she asked Georgie, as she finally got down a few gulps of the hot liquid and felt instantly more human.

"The Detective Inspector immediately took Harvey and Kitty into custody, I guess he's pretty sure they did it," Georgie answered, looking at the biscuits with longing.

"He arrested them, straight away?" Morgana was surprised.

"Well, no. I don't think so, he said he wanted to question them at the station, but that's almost the same, isn't it?"

"Mmm," Morgana said, as noncomitally as she was able. "Harvey is the obvious suspect, I mean, he must have been in the room?"

Georgie's eyes suddenly brightened with gossip. "Except he wasn't, he spent the night with Kitty. I saw him creeping down the hall at nearly midnight, and he wasn't back when Elise's maid went in."

Morgana's eyes widened. "That's taking a risk. What if Elise had woken up?"

Georgie shook her head. "Elise takes enough tranks to knock out an elephant at night. He probably thought he'd be back before Bonny came in, she wasn't supposed to wake them until eight. Goodness knows why she went in at half five, probably got confused with the time difference or jet lag or something."

"So, Harvey and Kitty were definitely having an affair? I guess that's a pretty good motive for murdering Elise? Though hardly the most subtle way to go about it."

"I know I would in their situation. She was such a cow to both of them. They probably took turns to stab her in her sleep," Georgie said with relish.

Morgana couldn't really picture the timid Kitty stabbing anyone, or Harvey either for that matter: he'd seemed almost afraid of his wife. But then, he'd probably been suppressing his feelings for years and they'd finally boiled over. She wondered if Elise had said something that had been the catalyst. It certainly was possible.

"Was there a Detective Sergeant here?" Morgana asked as casually as she could.

"Yes, I think his name's Treharne? He's in the library with Bernie, getting the low down on who we all are, I assume. He is seriously fit, fingers crossed that he wants to frisk me for the murder weapon or something." Georgie nudged Morgana, who tried not to look like she knew exactly what Georgie was saying. Being frisked by Tristan would certainly come high on her own wish list, even though it would probably be more like torture than anything else.

Not for the first time, Morgana felt a sharp stab of jealousy that Morwenna had got there first. Even though Tristan and Morwenna had dated back in school and broken up more than ten years ago, she could never go out with someone who'd had a relationship with her twin sister. But it didn't stop her from being attracted to him, no matter how hard she tried to eradicate the feelings.

She was brought out of her thoughts by Judy taking

her elbow. "Morwenna, dear, would you like to take a walk around the conservatory with me? His Lordship has a fine collection of plants, I believe."

Morgana looked at Judy in confusion. She had no particular interest in plants, unless of course they had some magical purpose, and she couldn't imagine that Judy did either. Judy responded by digging her fingers a little tighter into Morgana's arm, indicating that she had another purpose for wanting to go, so Morgana nodded, and reluctantly put down her unfinished coffee.

Together they walked out the back of the house, to a long room with a glass ceiling. Here, rows of flowers and seedling vegetables were set out in rows on tables, giving the air a wonderful earthy smell.

Judy cupped a geranium in her fingers. "Tell me, where is Morwenna?"

"She… I…" Morgana stopped and stared at Judy. "What do you mean?"

"Oh, don't look so worried, I'm not going to tell anyone. I just thought that with the police in the house it might be better if you told me the truth, so I know who I'm really dealing with, you understand?"

"How did you know?" Morgana asked, curiously.

"Her photo was taken a couple of weeks ago having dinner in a restaurant. She had bangs, dear, and you don't. While you might get your hair cut in that time, it isn't possible to grow it back that fast. And then I remembered reading once that she had an identical twin sister, which I assume is you?"

Morgana gave Judy a look of admiration. "You really don't miss anything, do you? You're right, of course. I'm Morgana. My sister didn't want to dupe anyone, but she had another engagement she couldn't get out of and Bernie insisted she came here otherwise she might lose the part. I hope he won't be too angry?"

Judy waved an airy hand. "Oh, he'll never notice."

"You're not going to tell him?" Morgana frowned in confusion.

"Why would I do that?"

"Well, he's your husband…"

"When he feels like it, or when I can be useful to him," Judy said, her mouth thinning into an angry line. "But knowing everyone's secrets is what gives me the edge."

"It's not much of a secret," she said, trying to diffuse the sudden tension in the room.

"No, it's not. But you'd be surprised at the things I know. Everyone has secrets, especially the people in this house. *Every single one of them.*"

"If you know something about the murder, you have to tell the police," Morgana said, feeling suddenly very wary of Judy's motives.

"I didn't say I knew anything about the murder, did I?" Judy gave a broad innocent smile and went back into the house, leaving Morgana to follow at a slower pace, feeling distinctly concerned.

Chapter Nine

"Oh, there you are!" Georgie came running toward Morgana. "The sexy sergeant is finished with Bernie and is asking to see *you* next. I've no idea why, you haven't done anything suspicious, have you?" Georgie looked delighted by the very idea.

"No," Morgana smiled back at her. "It's because he knows me, we grew up in the same village."

"Ooh, you lucky dog. Was he always that dreamy? Make sure you tell him that I'm single, see if you can drop it into the conversation?" Georgie gave Morgana a push towards the door at the other end of the drawing room. She went through it, and found herself in yet another drawing room. This one was smaller, with more furniture, and had a decidedly more welcome feeling to it. It was also empty, so she passed through it and opened the door far end, finding herself now in the library. She stopped short, and looked around in admiration. Books stretched from floor to ceiling. A small fire was lit in the grate, and four overstuffed leather armchairs were set around a large coffee table that held a chess set.

"Wow, I don't think I'd ever want to leave this room if I lived here."

Tristan stood up from one of the armchairs and gave her a tight smile. "Me either. Hello, Morwenna."

Morgana tilted her head giving him a once over. Tristan never wore a police uniform, instead favouring a suit and tie, but even the smart clothes couldn't diminish the impression she always carried of him. A bad boy in a leather jacket, the rebellious teenager who always caused trouble. The heartbreaker with a heart.

She knew she had to tell him the truth about who she really was, but that way he was looking at her at that moment was too intriguing to waste just yet. If he knew she was Morgana then he'd be more respectful, more cautious about crossing boundaries, nicer. But right now, he was regarding her in a whole new way and she was fascinated by it.

Tristan and Morwenna had a history. While Morgana might have thought herself in love with Tristan when she was fifteen and he was eighteen, Morwenna was the one who got him. She and her sister had fought over everything at that age, and Tristan was the big prize.

Tristan and Morwenna had been on again and off again for an entire year until they'd had a huge fight and Tristan had left the village, never to be seen again until he reappeared twelve years later as a police detective.

"Hello Tristan," Morgana said, adopting her best sashay as she made her way over to him. "You look good."

He raised one eyebrow and returned the once over in a far more intimate way than he normally looked at her. "You always look good, Morwenna. But you know that, don't you?"

Morgana felt attraction fizz in the air between them and knew she had to drop the act before it became any more personal. He thought he was talking to his ex-girlfriend, not to her sister.

But maybe just a little more? She tried to resist the temptation, then gave in to it. Moving to stand very close to him, she brushed some of his dark hair out of his eyes in a gesture she wouldn't normally dare to make. But

Morwenna would make it without a second thought.

He looked at her suspiciously. "Don't start, Morwenna. I'm here to work. It's too early for your brand of seduction."

"Am I starting something? You're the one looking at me like I'm exactly what you want for breakfast." She let her hand trail through his hair and down along his jawline. He'd shaved, despite the hour, and the freshness of his cologne seemed to invade her senses.

He caught hold of her wrist and brought it away from his face. "Don't use your magic powers on me, they stopped working a long time ago."

Morgana saw the haze of purple appear in his aura and knew he was lying. She could see his desire like a physical entity. She felt guilty, but it was just too much fun pushing his buttons to stop herself.

"But it was so good between us, every single time we made love, you begged for more," she goaded him, trying to use Morwenna's most sultry tone.

He looked down at her, humour dancing in his eyes at her provocative words. "I never begged, and I never thought of you again once I left. Perhaps, if you were *Morgana*, then maybe I'd beg you to help me now with my murder investigation, but *you* are no good to me at all, except maybe for this." He pulled her suddenly close and kissed her.

Morgana gasped, taken by surprise at the unexpected kiss. In an instant she was fifteen again, getting kissed for the very first time by Tristan. He'd thought she was Morwenna that time too. And just like the first time, she swayed into the kiss, wanting it with every fibre of her being. It took about three seconds for reality to reassert itself and she wrenched away, shoving him hard, then raising a hand to whack him on the arm.

"Morgana, stop! I'm sorry!" He was laughing hard as he ducked her hit.

Morgana froze, her arm still raised. "Wait…what did you call me?"

"It *is* you, isn't it?"

"How did you know? Was it the kiss, is it different?" She lowered her arm, unable to be mad at him when he was still laughing.

"No, I knew before then. Sorry, it was really unprofessional of me, I just couldn't resist when you kept pretending and I almost fell for it."

"Oh. So you were just trying to goad me when you said you'd want my help if I was Morgana?"

"Actually, I meant that bit. Are we good? Do you forgive me?"

Morgana was silent for a moment while she thought about it. He'd kissed her, knowing it was her. Should she read anything into that? It was just a kiss, and a pretty tame one at that, just lips pressed against each other. Plus, they'd known each other most of their lives, it probably meant nothing. She felt slightly depressed by that but quickly squelched the feeling.

"Morwenna would be furious if she knew," Morgana said with a grin.

"Well, I'm not telling if you don't. Not that it's any of her business these days anyway. Though I probably shouldn't have done it while on duty."

Did that mean that he thought it was okay when *not* on duty? Her eyes met his, and she tried to get a read on his feelings.

"Don't," Tristan said, looking away and into the fire.

"Don't what?"

"Don't try to read my aura. You've already seen my soul, you know I'm beyond hope. I don't have any trust left in me."

This was true. She had once viewed Tristan using her third eye, which showed her the very being of whoever she was looking at. But to do it came at great cost and she'd been left shaking and blind for a good while afterwards. Tristan's soul had shocked her. It was like looking at the night sky. Almost completely dark with pinpricks of light shining out. And his heart... it had been like a black hole, just empty. The strangest thing of all, though, had been the white crown of light that circled his head. She'd never seen anything like it.

Tristan cleared his throat to break the silence that seemed to stretch between them. "So, what do you think? Will you help me with this case? I'd value your opinion on the other people here."

"I will, on one condition. Can we keep up the pretence that I'm Morwenna? Judy Gossard knows the truth, but I'd rather keep it quiet from the rest if at all possible?"

"If that's what you want."

"Isn't this a straight-forward case though? I thought DI Lowen had already taken Harvey and Kitty away for questioning?"

Tristan rolled his shoulders to show he wasn't sure. "They are the most likely suspects, but to be honest, it could have been anyone. From what Bernie Gossard has told me, it sounds as though Elise Everett had a lot of people who might want her dead. Georgiana Grace, for example, Bernie says she would get the lead role if Elise broke her contract. And Bernie himself admits he never wanted Elise for the part, she was forced on him by the money man behind the movie."

"Dickie Magnus?"

"That's the one, it's suspicious that he insisted on this get-together and then isn't here." Tristan suddenly became very formal as he sat down in one of the armchairs and opened his notebook.

Morgana took the chair opposite him. "It's even more suspicious," she said, "because he told Bernie that he couldn't get away from Los Angeles to be here, but Georgie says she saw him on the same plane to London as her."

"Interesting." Tristan made a note of that. "I'll get someone to check into his movements. Is there anything you can tell me about the others? I don't suppose anyone has a convenient aura of rage around them?" He quirked her another smile.

Not for the first time, Morgana thought how nice it was to be with someone who knew about her weird talents and just accepted them. But she shook her head. "I locked down my abilities before I came here. It just seemed daft to have my senses wide open when meeting so many new people."

He regarded her thoughtfully. "It takes a lot out of you, doesn't it, doing what you can do?"

"Yes, it's not as bad as opening my third eye but still pretty draining. If I'm open then I can't filter it, I feel it all. Anger, sadness, fear, loneliness, annoyance."

"Nothing positive?"

"You'd be surprised how little of that people have

when around others. But those emotions too, yes. Joy, hope, gratitude, pride, contentment. That kind of thing."

"Love?" He looked interested.

"Definitely love," she smiled. "And let's not forget lust."

"Certainly not. But murder isn't generally driven by lust. Love, hate, revenge, or money are the motives we look for. How would you feel about trying to read the others if we brought them in just one at a time?"

"Sure," she agreed. "But they're going to think it's really weird that I'm helping you. I'm playing the part of Morwenna, remember? I'm an actress with no magical ability. At least as Morgana everyone knows I'm a witch, but Morwenna keeps her powers hidden and pretends to be normal."

"Well, could you do it from behind the curtain or something?" Tristan looked over at the heavy red velvet drapes that were pushed to the edges of the windows.

"Seriously?" Morgana couldn't help but smile at the image of herself popping out from behind the curtain to signal to Tristan. "I'm going to feel ridiculous hiding there, and what if someone spots me? Plus I need to be able to see them, remember?"

Tristan rubbed at his chin. "How about you do it just for the ones who might have difficulty accepting you as a Police Consultant? Or the ones who are particularly nervous?"

Morgana walked over to the curtains and slipped behind them to see how practical it was. "Actually, this could work, they are quite threadbare on the back, there's a hole here, and if you moved the other chair a bit to the right then I'd have a clear side view of both you and the interviewee." She came back out, brushing some dust off her jumper, and plopped back into the armchair opposite him. "The other problem is that they're going to be guarded. Talking to the police tends to make most people put up barriers, and I can't see through them. Sometimes people are weak-willed and easy to read, but I don't think you'll find much of that in this house. Lots of strong personalities."

"We'll just have to do our best. So, where shall we start? I've got a list here of everyone in the house."

Morgana looked over it. "This isn't everyone, what about the Baroness?"

"Who?" Tristan looked confused.

"The Dowager Baroness of Latheborne, she lives here too. She went to bed as soon as the lights went out last night. I haven't seen her since."

"Hmm, we'll have to find out more about her, is she a likely suspect?" Tristan brought out a notepad and wrote down the name.

"Not really, she's about ninety! Then again, she seemed a tough old bird to me, and I know from experience never to underestimate old ladies."

"Noted," Tristan said, actually making a note. "In the meantime, shall we do them alphabetically?"

Morgana twisted her lip. "Do we have to? That means starting with Ethan Cope and I'm trying to avoid him. It seems he and Morwenna might have been an item recently and he wants to pick up where they left off."

Tristan choked back a laugh. "Oh, Morgana. The things you have to do for your sister!"

"I know, right?" she agreed.

Tristan shook his head at her stupidity. He knew only too well how manipulative Morwenna could be at getting her own way. "Thankfully, it's not Ethan Cope yet, you forgot Adams. Courtney Adams would be first on an alphabetical list. I've got the staff on a separate list, here." He handed it over.

"Oh, yes. Adams would be a good place to start because as a butler he probably notices all the small things. Plus being the only one in the room who was stone-cold sober."

"Hit the drinks hard, did you?" Tristan grinned.

"Well, it was flowing fairly freely, yes." She ran her eye over the second list. "Bonny, Elise's maid, and Louise, the housemaid, and Mrs. Brown, the Housekeeper. You should probably ask Lord Latheborne about them before you question them?"

"I've already spoken to Miss Bonny Santos, as she was the one who found the victim, but even though I don't think she did it, I did get the impression she was hiding something from me, so perhaps we could talk to her again. But I agree, we should probably get some back history from Lord Latheborne before we meet the rest of the staff. Is he someone you need to keep yourself hidden for?"

"Definitely. He dislikes me."

Tristan raised both eyebrows. "Does he, now? What did you do to annoy him, pass the salt the wrong way?"

"Oh, shut up." Morgana heaved herself out of the comfortable armchair and stepped back behind the curtain carefully, trying not to make it move.

Tristan pulled a radio from his pocket and spoke into it. "Cartwright? I'm ready to start talking to the other guests. Could you bring Lord Latheborne to the Library?" He put it away and looked toward Morgana. "You ready?"

Morgana closed her eyes and relaxed her body as she worked on opening her mind. She'd put up a lot of mental barriers and they needed taking down one at a time. After two or three minutes had passed she opened her eyes again and found the hole in the curtain to peer through.

"I'm ready."

Chapter Ten

Tristan was extremely good at controlling his emotions, probably as a direct result of the work he did, Morgana surmised. But if she concentrated hard enough then she could usually pick up a small amount of shading around him. Seeing auras wasn't an exact science, but certain emotions gave off certain colours. She couldn't tell from an aura if someone was good or bad, she'd need to open her third eye to do that, but she could see what they were feeling at that exact moment in time.

Tristan had a brightness pulsing around him. His posture was relaxed but his aura said he was on high alert. She also noticed a slight tint of purple still lingered at the edges.

Purple was attraction, lust.

Had he actually been as affected by their brief kiss as she was?

Constable Cartwright knocked once and then entered the room with Lord Latheborne. Cartwright took up a stance at the door, and Tristan gestured to Lord Latheborne that he should join him at the coffee table.

Morgana was actually glad to get the opportunity to view Lord Latheborne aura. In her quieter moments, she had wondered what she'd see. Now she knew, it was the same lovely dark blue as his eyes. Honest, but wary. *He doesn't trust easily*, she reflected. It lightened towards the edges of the circle around him, turning orange, indicating good health. *Well, that one was pretty obvious anyway*, she thought, admiring his physique and feeling a bit like a grubby voyeur as she allowed herself to properly check him out in a way she'd never do if he could see her.

"Let's get the obvious questions out of the way first, Lord Latheborne," Tristan said, bringing Morgana's attention back to the point of the interview. "Can you tell me your movements last night, who you were with, and what time you went to bed?"

Lord Latheborne leaned back in his chair looking thoughtful. "After dinner, I came in here with Bernie and Ethan. We had some drinks, talked for a while, Bernie went up at around ten-thirty, Ethan and I a short while later."

"Did anyone leave at all during the time you spend in here?"

"No," Lord Latheborne said decisively.

"Did you see anyone else when you went upstairs?"

"It was difficult to, as there was a power cut last night. Anyone could have been prowling about in the dark unnoticed if they weren't carrying a candle. But no, the only person I saw, apart from Bernie and Ethan, was Morwenna. She was going back to her room from the bathroom, somewhere between eleven o'clock and midnight." Lord Latheborne's expression darkened, reminding Morgana of their awkward conversation the night before.

Tristan finished writing some notes and then turned the page on his pad.

"What do you think of Miss Emrys?" Tristan asked, a little too blandly.

Morgana ground her teeth, knowing he was just posing the question to provoke her.

"I think she's typical of her profession. Beautiful, but ambitious at the cost of others."

Morgana drew in an insulted breath. When had she *ever* given him that impression?

"She's a social climber, just like the rest of them," Lord Latheborne continued. "Yet…" he trailed off.

Tristan waited expectantly, but Lord Latheborne only shook his head. "I don't know, she's surprising, sometimes."

Morgana could see that Tristan was longing to turn and look her way to see her reaction, but he managed to restrain himself. "I'd like to know a little more about your staff. How long they've been with you, and where they were before, that kind of thing?"

"They're not involved in all this," Lord Latheborne said, firmly. "Adams is the grandson of my previous butler, and he trained at Buckingham Palace, have you any idea how rigorous their scrutiny is there? You won't find anyone with more impeccable credentials. Louise grew up right here at the manor. Her father is the groundskeeper. They live behind the house in the stable block, which has been converted now. Mrs. Brown locks all the doors once Louise leaves for the night, so she wasn't even in the manor when it happened."

"And what about Mrs. Brown?"

"She came from an agency, I think. I can get Adams to dig out their details. There's no connection to Elise Everett though, and Mrs. Brown has been here nearly six months."

Tristan pushed a piece of paper across the table to Lord Latheborne. "I have a list of the people in the house given to me by Bernie Gossard, is there anyone missing?"

Lord Latheborne glanced over it and gave a chuckle.

"Yes, my grandmother. Lady Olivia Westley, Dowager Baroness of Latheborne. Overlook her at your peril, she's still a force to be reckoned with. However, she went to bed early and has chosen not to leave it as yet. I checked in on her this morning and she said she couldn't be bothered with all the fuss of murder and would take her meals in her room until everyone leaves."

"It's unlikely then that she may have witnessed anything?" Tristan asked.

"Her bedroom is on the ground floor at the back, she can't manage the stairs anymore, so no, it's not possible that she saw anything at all." He gave Tristan a stern look as though warning him not to pursue it.

Tristan nodded in acceptance. "What is your opinion on the other guests? Is there anyone at all that you think has been acting suspiciously?"

Lord Latheborne gave a humourless laugh. "I don't think my opinion would be very valid. It's fairly negative across the board. I don't like subterfuge or acting, I think the world would be better if everyone was a bit more sincere."

Morgana shifted uncomfortably at these words. In general, she completely agreed with them, but it was hard not to feel like they were directed solely at herself. He would despise her even more if he found out she was there under false pretences.

"I'm also not a particular fan of movies," he continued. "I don't even watch a lot of television. I prefer books. But in terms of acting suspiciously, then yes, I've seen something."

"Such as?" Tristan straightened in his chair.

"The maid, Bonny. I'm in the room next door to

Elise, so I was the first there when Bonny started screaming. She calmed down a bit when I came in, and then rushed over to the dressing table and started going through the jewellery. When I asked what she was doing she said she wanted to make sure nothing had been stolen. But that's rather a strange thing to care about at that moment, or it is in my opinion anyway."

"Interesting." Tristan nodded his head, making another note. "Have you ever met Elise or had any connection to her prior to this weekend?" Tristan stopped writing and fixed Lord Latheborne with a very direct stare.

"No."

"Thank you for your time." Tristan rose to his feet to indicate the interview was over.

"Well?" Tristan looked at the curtains as the door closed behind Lord Latheborne.

She emerged, pushed a small spider off her shoulder, and shrugged. "So far as I can tell, he's being completely truthful. He keeps his emotions on tight control, but his aura is blue. I'd say he's clean."

"He has no motive either, so far as we can tell. I'd say he was a man of good instincts, so shall we follow his suspicion and talk to Bonny next?"

Morgana was slightly peeved that Tristan believed Lord Latheborne to be a man of good instincts, especially as Lord Latheborne had made some rather scathing observations about *her*, but she said nothing and gave a brief nod of agreement.

Unfortunately, she too thought Lord Latheborne had good instincts.

In fact, as loathe as she was to admit it, she thought

Lord Latheborne had pretty good *everything*.

Chapter Eleven

"Cartwright?" Tristan addressed the constable who still stood at the door. "We'll have Miss Santos again, please."

A minute later the maid came in and took the seat across from Tristan. Morgana squinted her through the hole in the curtain, examining the girl's aura. She saw hints of green, which indicated duplicity. Morgana wanted to tell Tristan this, but she knew he was smart enough to pick up on something so obvious by himself.

"Just a few more questions, Bonny, nothing to worry about," Tristan said, in a soothing voice. "I just want to clear up exactly what happened and when."

"It wasn't me." The girl looked terrified.

"Of course not, I'm more interested in why you went into her room?"

"It is my job to wake her each day."

"At five-thirty? That was about the time you went in, wasn't it?" Tristan made a show of looking at his notes.

"I...I not know, I was confused. No, I normally wake her at eight o'clock. Much shaking, she take pills, make her keep sleeping if I don't wake."

"So, you went in early by mistake?"

"Yes, is so." The girl nodded eagerly. "But realise mistake, Mr. Everett not there, Mrs. Everett not take pills. I was about to leave when I see blood."

"Right." Tristan looked at his notes again. "Then you screamed for help. But we have a witness that says that once help arrived on the scene you went over to Mrs. Everett's jewel case and began to check it. Can you explain that to me?"

Morgana's eyes widened as Bonny's aura instantly changed colour. It was suddenly thick with yellow clouds.

Whatever she says next, it's a lie, Morgana thought.

"Mrs. Everett have issue with missing items. Someone stealing from her. I think maybe she murdered for her diamonds. I think police will want to know this and go to see."

"Really?" Tristan sounded as sceptical as Morgana felt. "And was there anything missing?"

"No, all there." Bonny was firm in her reply.

Morgana saw Tristan scribble something, and guessed he was going to get someone to check the jewel case and see if anything had been removed from it.

"Just one last question, Miss. Santos. Have you seen anyone acting strangely at all? Or coming and going in a suspicious way?"

Bonny brightened and leaned forward. "Yes, yes. I can help. I see what the rich not see. I see the other side of the door. The maid, she is rude and not know her place, acting like it her own house, I am sure she is mistress of the Lord Latheborne. And the Housekeeper, she is liar, she pretend she is old and her back is bad so that other staff do all her work and lift heavy things for her, she is lazy, and wear too much make-up, she too want to be his mistress I think."

"I see." Tristan looked at her doubtfully.

"And the Butler, he not sleep in his bed, he sneaking around the house. I see him going downstairs when I get up, I think he ghost in just white shirt." Bonny paused as an idea struck her. "He was coming from Mrs. Everett's room! He murder her!"

Tristan glanced up sharply. "You saw him? You saw him leave her room just before you went in?"

"Yes, yes." Bonny looked excited now.

Tristan glanced at the window where Morgana was hiding, making her aware he wanted her to pay particular attention at that moment. "Thank you, Miss. Santos, you've been most helpful." He gestured that she could leave.

The maid curtseyed and went, seemingly happy.

"You didn't believe a word of what she said, did you?" Morgana commented, sticking her head around the curtain.

"Not really, but she did seem quite sure that she'd seen Carlton Adams. That detail about him coming downstairs in only his shirt, it's unlikely she has the imagination to make that up."

"I suppose so," Morgana conceded.

"But I highly doubt that either the maid or the housekeeper are Lord Latheborne's mistresses, he doesn't seem the type." Tristan smiled.

"It has been known to happen." Morgana couldn't resist the jab at her unwelcoming host.

"Huh, and there was me, under the impression that he only had eyes for you," Tristan teased her.

"Yep, he's looking at me and hoping I'm next, he dislikes me intently," Morgana snapped.

"I think you'll find he doesn't, which is what annoys him so much," Tristan said, lightly.

Morgana scowled at him. "I'm the one reading people here, don't go trying to be perceptive, especially when it comes to me."

"Hit a nerve, did I?" Tristan gave her a side glance

before asking Constable Cartwright to send in Carlton Adams.

Carlton Adams looked impeccable as he walked serenely into the library. Morgana saw him giving Tristan the once over, and a barely perceptible smile of approval touched the corner of his lips. Morgana tried to hide her own smile as she wondered if the approval was for Tristan's very sharp suit, or for the man himself.

"Mr Adams," Tristan began, once Adams had taken the time to sit carefully perched on the edge of the opposite chair. "I'll get straight to the point as I'm sure you're very busy with so many guests in the house."

"That would be appreciated," Adams said, looking even more approving.

"One of the other people in the house feels sure they saw you coming out of Mrs Everett's bedroom shortly before she was found murdered."

Adams looked affronted and aghast, his hand going to his chest. "I never!" He exclaimed. "I didn't go near her room."

"I see, but you were up and about at that time? In the corridor perhaps?" Tristan probed.

Adams pursed his lips. "It's true, someone may have seen me, but I was just checking all the candles had been properly doused."

Tristan gave him a sympathetic look. "In just your shirt? We both know you wouldn't dream of performing your duties half-dressed. I believe you weren't in Elise's bedroom, but you were in someone else's?" It was probably nothing more than an educated guess, but Morgana could immediately see Tristan had been right. Adams, however, tightened his lips and went mute.

"Adams, you must tell me, we won't share the information with the other guests or your employer," Tristan tried to reassure him. But Adams merely gave a firm single shake of his head.

"Very well," Tristan said, patiently. "Can you at least tell us if you saw anything suspicious, or anyone else moving about that night?"

Adams regarded him for a long moment as though weighing up what to say. "Very well," he replied finally. "I did as it happens. I saw Mr Gossard coming up the stairs at about a quarter past five this morning."

"From where?" Tristan wrote fast on his notepad.

"If I had to guess, then I'd say the Billiard Room. I noticed it was disturbed when I did the rounds after breakfast. I check every room downstairs and there was a dent in the seat cushions. To my knowledge, the room hasn't been used this weekend."

"Any idea what he might have been doing in there?"

Adams gave them a prim look. "I couldn't possibly say."

Tristan waited until Adams left the room, then turned to Morgana, who was already pushing the curtains aside in relief.

"Was it just me or was he implying that Bernie Gossard went to meet a woman?"

She nodded in agreement, practically falling into the armchair beside Tristan's. "That's how it sounded to me. But who?"

"Elise, perhaps? Maybe the whole thing is a lovers' quarrel gone wrong?" Tristan suggested.

Morgana remembered the way Bernie had been towards Elise and gave a doubtful lift of her shoulders.

"I don't think he liked her very much."

"It seems like no one liked her, but it doesn't mean he objected to sleeping with her."

"Maybe." She still didn't think it at all likely.

"Let's ask him."

Morgana's energy felt very low now, but she heaved herself reluctantly to her feet. "I definitely have to hide for this one. Apart from Ethan, he's the only person in the house who actually knows Morwenna. He wouldn't get me being here at all."

"You sure you're up to it? You do look a bit pale." Tristan caught hold of her hand as she moved past him.

She smiled down at him. His hand on hers was gentle but she instantly found herself accidentally absorbing some of his strength. She wouldn't normally but her senses were wide open at that moment and her gift was crying out for more energy to keep working. He had plenty to spare and so she tightened her grip and deliberately drew from it. Her posture straightened. Tristan's energy was potent, she could feel the brightness of it coursing through her, but also his darkness. Flashes of his thoughts or memories came unwanted. Black walls closing in around her, bars on a small dirty window, unwashed smells, someone screaming in the distance.

She released his hand abruptly, horrified by the nightmarish insight to his mind.

"What?" Tristan asked, seeing her face.

"Nothing." She took a deep breath. "I'm ready now."

He gave her a long look and then nodded. "Cartwright? Can you send Mr. Gossard back in?"

Chapter Twelve

"Mr Gossard," Tristan began.

"I told you, you must call me Bernie, I only want to help." Bernie leaned back in the armchair and lit a cigar. Morgana tried not to wince at what it might do to the books around them, but she supposed they'd probably already been exposed to generations of cigar smoke or pipe smoke. Behind the curtain, she too attempted to relax and to tune into Bernie's aura.

It was orange with confidence and vitality, but she caught the wafts of green pass through it and knew he had something to hide.

"I'm glad to hear you say that because I need to ask you an awkward question." Tristan kept his tone formal. "Could you explain why you were in the Billiard Room last night, and how long you were there? And more importantly, who you were with?"

Bernie paused mid-movement just as he was sucking on his cigar, then promptly started coughing.

Tristan shot Morgana a quick look of satisfaction while Bernie's attention was diverted.

"Who told you that?" Bernie demanded when he'd regained his composure.

"It's not relevant, but we know you were there, and we know you came upstairs at around the same time as we suspect the murder was committed, so it would be a very good idea if you told the truth unless you want to be arrested too?"

Morgana was surprised at the amount of pressure Tristan was putting on the other man when he'd been quite gentle with the suspects so far, but she supposed he must have a game plan of sorts or a good idea of how to handle different types of personality. She wondered if it was a skill she could learn.

"I was alone. I simply wanted some quiet time. My wife snores, you know, but don't tell her I said that. It's all those pills she takes I think. We're both fairly insomniac, apparently having an active mind is a sign of high intelligence, or so I've been told. But she medicates to get her sleep, whereas I use the time to work."

"You're saying you were working? At five in the morning, in the Billiard Room?" Tristan raised one sceptical eyebrow.

"Yes, just planning out scenes, that kind of thing."

"And you were alone?" Tristan asked, his voice containing just a hint of disbelief.

"Yes." Bernie was adamant.

"Every moment? Are you absolutely sure?" Tristan applied more pressure.

Morgana gave Tristan a silent cheer for tenacity. The lie had been so clear to her that she supposed he must have seen it too.

Bernie got to his feet, looking outraged. "Be very sure where you're going with this, Detective. I'm a married man. I was alone, got it?"

Tristan made a calming gesture with his hand. "I'm sure that you saw someone else," he said, carefully. "There were other people moving about the house last night. Anything you can tell us would be very useful."

Bernie eyed him warily but eventually, his stance relaxed a little and he sat back down.

"I didn't see anyone when I came upstairs, but I did see someone when I went down if that's any help?"

"Absolutely," Tristan said, once again putting pen to paper. "We haven't actually established time of death so any movements at all that you can provide could be key."

"I doubt this will help because the person I saw was Elise herself. It must have been around midnight, she was leaving her room and I had to wait for her to go past before I left mine. Didn't want to get trapped talking to her, you know?"

"Did you see where she was going?" Tristan made rapid notes.

"Oh yes," Bernie nodded, smugly. "She went into Ethan Cope's bedroom. Just walked straight in and shut the door behind her. They must know each other better than anyone suspected. Not that I'm suggesting he killed her, he's too smart to ruin his opportunities with a murder charge. Young actor like that, with so much potential, well, that would be incredibly stupid, he's got too much ahead of him to risk it."

"I see." Tristan rubbed at his temples as though he were getting a headache. "Anyone else?"

"No, don't think so. But if you want to know who murdered that bloody woman then you should ask my wife, she always knows everything."

"Thank you, we'll do that." Tristan's smile was taut as he shut his notebook to let Bernie know the interview was over.

Tristan stood and stretched out his tall frame. "Do you ever feel like you're paddling upstream? That lot really don't like to share." He walked over to the window to stand beside Morgana and stared vacantly out over the lawns.

"I was expecting you to be a bit more pushy," Morgana said, giving him an appraising look. "Can't you just force them to tell you? Aren't they like, legally obliged to, or something?"

"That's not how we do it. First, we find out who was where in a non-accusatory way. We narrow it down before we start applying the thumbscrews."

"So, pretend to be their friend and let them open up and then trip up?" Morgana said, quizzically.

"Not exactly." He turned his back on the view outside. "Everyone, except the murderer, is innocent. They don't deserve to be treated as suspects, even though they are."

"You're just a big softie," she teased.

He frowned. "No. I just have an overdeveloped sense of justice. *No one* should be made to feel like they did anything wrong unless they really did."

Morgana thought about what she'd seen in Tristan's mind and softened her voice. "That's what happened to you, isn't it? You were accused of something?"

"I was set up, yes. But this isn't about me." Tristan turned his back again, focussing on the view once more.

"*This* isn't. But I'd like to know. Something big happened and it changed you." Morgana knew she should leave it alone. It really wasn't any of her business. But she couldn't.

Tristan rolled his neck. "I was arrested, convicted, and sentenced for murder. It was overturned, that's all there is to it. It was a good thing, really. I wasn't on a great path and you're right, it changed things. After that, I wanted to be a force for good, to get the bad guys, and be sure, *very* sure, I always had the right man—" he looked over his shoulder with a grin "–or woman."

Morgana saw his aura darken with bad memories. "How long?" She asked, knowing he'd understand exactly what she meant.

"Nearly two years," he said, his voice empty.

"I'm so sorry," she said, feeling the pain coming off him. Nearly two years in prison for a crime he didn't commit? It was a miracle that he'd decided to become a police officer after that, he could so easily have gone the other way and been driven by anger instead of justice.

"Did they get the person who really did it?" She had to ask.

"Yes. She's serving multiple life sentences now." Tristan's eyes stared at something she couldn't see.

"You loved her," she stated.

"And you are too nosy for your own good." Tristan made an effort to relax his stance. "Come on, I have a feeling it's going to be a long day of interviews. Are you ready for the next one?"

"I guess so." Morgana sat down and let her head flop back against the chair. Tristan's energy had given her a temporary boost, but it was already waning. "I wouldn't say no to a cup of tea first," she admitted.

"Cartwright?" Tristan raised his voice and the officer outside the door immediately opened it. "Can you see if we could get a pot of tea in here? Then give us twenty minutes before sending in Ethan Cope?"

Morgana closed her eyes to avoid further mental exertions and rested while Tristan summarised to her what they'd already learned. Mrs. Brown came and went bringing some very welcome tea and a walnut cake, which did a great deal to revive them both.

"Okay to carry on, now? Let's try and narrow down who was with who, where, and when," Tristan said with determination.

"I think I'll stay seated for the next couple, or I'm going to be no use to you later," Morgana said.

"Is that so?" Tristan gave her a look she could only have described as *insinuating*, and Morgana stuck her tongue out at him in response.

"But if Ethan knows Morwenna?" He let the question hang.

"I'll have to tell him the truth at some point anyway, especially as they run in the same circles. I think he can keep his mouth shut."

Ethan Cope sauntered into the room looking relaxed and confident.

"I say, this is all very dramatic, isn't it?" He said, seating himself opposite them as though enthusiastic to be questioned. "Why are *you* here, Morwenna?"

Tristan spoke before she could. "Miss Emrys has some experience with this kind of situation and has in fact consulted for the police in the past. She has a talent for seeing things that others don't."

Morgana noticed that Tristan had cleverly used her last name instead of her first so that he didn't need to openly refer to her as either Morwenna or Morgana. She'd actually only 'consulted' for the police once, when asked to look at a suspect with her third eye to see if they'd recently committed murder. It wasn't an experience she had ever intended to repeat.

"Really?" Ethan looked highly amused. "I had no idea, Morwenna. What a very exciting double life you lead."

Morgana gave him a tight smile. "It's not something I do often. I'm just helping out as I was here."

"Strange second string for an actress though?" Ethan regarded her with curiosity.

Tristan cleared his throat, drawing Ethan's attention to himself.

"We just had a couple of questions for you about your movements last night. It seems that Mrs. Everett was seen going into your bedroom last night at about midnight. Can you tell us a little more about that?"

"It's not what you think." Ethan gave Morgana an apologetic glance. "Well, it is, but it was one-sided. She gave me quite a shock, to be honest. I thought it might be you, Morwenna, waiting until my uncle had gone to his room, so imagine my surprise when Elise Everett breezed in as though I'd be grateful for her attention or something! She was a vile hag, and tried to blackmail me into sleeping with her." He pulled a disgusted face.

"Blackmail you with what?" Tristan asked, feigning only casual interest.

Morgana watched as Ethan's aura changed from an open blue to a dark red of anger. She tried to keep her face impassive but her instinct was to recoil away from him. It was a level of malevolence she'd never have expected in him.

Ethan was silent for so long that Morgana didn't think he was going to answer, but eventually, he said, "I first met Elise two years ago at a party, I was there with a friend. He happened to be working with her at the time, and we went over to say hello. We stayed for a couple of drinks and then we left the party and went our separate ways. I got safely home in a taxi but apparently, he decided he was sober enough to drive. They pulled his car out of the river the next day and found enough drugs in his system to have killed him even if he hadn't had the accident."

"She thought you'd given him the drugs?" Tristan asked.

"Worse. She said she *saw* me put them into his drink, that she'd make sure everyone knew the truth." Ethan stared at the floor, his fingers curling into tight fists.

"A nasty rumour to weather," Tristan said, softly, "but why would anyone believe it?"

"Because it was Jack Macy. He was going to play Darwin, but I got the role instead after he died."

"I see. So she tried to blackmail you. How did you react?"

"I told her to sling her hook. I said she could do her worst." He raised his face, cold fury stark in his features.

"But you were very angry," Morgana said, knowing Tristan would pick up on the fact she could see it.

"I was bloody livid! And you know why? Because I think *she* was the one who spiked his glass that night. Jack didn't take drugs. He liked a drink or two, but that was it. They'd just wrapped up making The Dark of Night, and because of his death and all the hype it meant that the film did way better than it should have. It was an average performance at best, but suddenly it was being hailed as a cult hit. *She* was the one who benefited."

Tristan considered this information for a moment then asked, "Do you believe that Elise was capable of premeditated murder?"

Ethan gave a cold smile. "Haven't you heard all the stories yet? I'd have thought everyone would be falling over themselves to tell you. There are numerous 'accidents' that happened to people around her."

"Thank you, we'll certainly look into that." Tristan made a note on his pad. "So, how long was Elise in your room last night?"

"A few minutes at most. I showed her out and watched until she went down the corridor and back to her own door. I didn't trust her, you see."

Morgana noticed that Ethan's fingernails were still digging into his palms and the way the red mist of his aura swirled around him. He had definitely *wanted* to kill her even if he hadn't done it.

"Did you see anyone else?" Tristan said, almost resigned to further tangles in the web.

"Yes, actually. I saw Georgie coming up the main staircase. I didn't wait to see where she was heading though, I'd had my fill of them all by then!" He suddenly looked very young to Morgana, and she felt rather sorry for him. Despite the arrogance and self-assuredness that he seemed to have, he was probably out of his depth with all these predatory older women. It was just as well, for his sake, that Morwenna *hadn't* been there after all. She'd have had him for breakfast.

"Well, well," Tristan said, once Ethan had left the room. "The revelations just keep coming."

"Yes, and the suspects too. I suppose that means we have to interview Georgie next?"

"I'm afraid so. Is there anyone who just stayed in their own bed do you think?" Tristan raised a teasing eyebrow at her.

"I did," she replied tartly.

"Hmm, you weren't tempted to visit Ethan

yourself?"

"While pretending to be Morwenna? How twisted do you think I am?" She glowered.

"You flirted with me while pretending to be her."

"Yes, but that's different, it's you…" She trailed off, not quite sure how to finish the sentence so that it didn't sound bad. "You know I'd never do anything like that with Ethan. It's just you and I have history, I mean, you and she have history…" She stopped again, feeling her cheeks redden.

Please, please, don't pursue it, she thought. *I'm an adult now, I grew out of being in love with you when we were teenagers and you chose my sister.* But she knew she was just lying to herself. She'd always have a weakness for Tristan Treharne, and it wasn't going to go away. *If anything, it's stronger now than it was then!* Morgana gave her inner voice a metaphorical push off a cliff. *Shut up, you're making my face give away too much.*

Tristan smiled knowingly at her embarrassed expression and mercifully changed the subject. "Do you think Ethan did it? You looked kind of horrified at whatever it was you could see in his aura."

Morgana exhaled with relief. "You caught that, did you? You're right, he wanted to murder her, and he definitely believed she deserved it, but I didn't sense any lies at all. I think he told us the truth about what happened, both in the past and last night."

"And was Elise really capable of bumping off her co-stars to further her career?"

"I can't say for sure, I never looked at her aura. But from the short time I spent with her, I'd say it was entirely possible."

"Which means the motives keep coming."

"Yes. In fact, most of them had just as much reason as Harvey and Kitty. I know it seems cut and dried, but I truly don't think it was either of them." She thought back on how they had behaved after the murder and decided it wasn't some guilty performance.

"Why not?" Tristan went alert with interest.

"I don't know. Just a sense. The murderer is still in the house."

"I really hope that you're wrong," he said, looking concerned.

"Well, we know Georgiana Grace had beef with Elise. Elise was threatened by Georgie, I think, and she definitely tried to smear her at some point, but Georgie seems over that. It's possible she did something even more awful to her that we haven't heard about yet? I assume she's our next witness to question?"

Tristan nodded, "Yes. Another actress, let's just hope she's not cut from the same cloth as Elise or Morwenna for that matter."

"I like Georgie," Morgana said, "and you should know that she did ask me to tell you that she's single, if you happen to decide you don't mind actresses after all."

Tristan only groaned in response.

Chapter Thirteen

Georgie's aura was vibrant. Health and vitality shone out of her, almost making Morgana smile. She didn't know if her new friend was a killer or not, but she knew that, at this particular moment, Georgie was almost bouncing in her chair at the idea of being questioned.

"This is so cool, Morwenna, you and the hot cop both grilling me together. It's like Steed and Peel from The Avengers or something."

"Feels more like the X-Files to me sometimes," Tristan muttered, giving Morgana an amused look. "Only, I'm the sane one."

Morgana tutted at him and gave Georgie her best serious look. "Georgie, I know you're not sad about Elise, but you must realise that makes you a suspect?"

"No way! I thought Harvey and Kitty did it? That's what everyone is saying." Georgie was wide-eyed with interest.

"We haven't ruled anyone out at this stage," Tristan tried his best to insert a dampener into his voice.

"Awesome. Can I be played by someone totally gorgeous when this becomes a screenplay of its own? I don't want to play myself, I want to do Elise, I could make her utterly *gruesome*." Georgie clasped her hands together looking thrilled at the very idea.

"When you came to my room last night, you were on your way to meet someone, weren't you?" Morgana asked as she watched Georgie make eyes at Tristan.

"Is that what I said? I think I was mistaken." Georgie suddenly looked shifty.

"Georgie!" Morgana said, exasperated.

"I'm sorry, I can't confirm or deny that." Georgie looked stubborn.

Tristan held up a hand. "It's fine, you don't have to. But you were seen coming up the stairs shortly after midnight, and we know Elise was also wondering about at that time. I don't suppose you saw her, did you?"

Georgie's enthusiasm returned and she nodded vigorously. "I did! I remember now. She was knocking on Keefe's door."

"Keefe Mohan's room? Are you sure?" Tristan shot a look at Morgana, and then made some notes. "Did she go into his room?"

"No. I wasn't close enough to hear everything but I did hear them arguing. She said she was going to tell the press who was in his bedroom with him or something like that, and he said they'd talk about it later. I saw him bang his door shut and I saw her face, she looked angry, but sort of pleased with herself at the same time, know what I mean?"

"And then?"

"That's it. I hurried to my room before she could see me. I swear I didn't leave again until all the screaming started."

"I seem to remember you saying that Elise tried to destroy your career when you first started getting some good roles?" Morgana put in.

"And then some." Georgie nodded vigorously again. "That woman was a viper. She'd come over oh so nice and then bam!" She shot out her hand miming a snake attack. "She put a wedge under the door of a girl's dressing room this one time, so the girl totally missed her cue and got fired. But it wasn't one way, there was this poor runner who she yelled at and he put laxatives in her drink. Unfortunately, it had no effect at all so far as we know, but I think it's because she takes them morning, noon, and night anyway. But she was vile to some makeup woman who did manage to get revenge by putting itching powder in her wig, apparently, it was hysterical, I just wish I'd been there. Still, it was mostly harmless pranking, not murder."

"Not that harmless if you lose your job though." Tristan didn't return her grin.

"No." Georgie sobered. "I guess I was lucky. She went to the press and told them a lot of lies about me. I was engaged at the time and my fiancée broke it off after that, so I was pretty upset and I know how it feels, but I didn't let her beat me."

"Do you know if there is anyone else here who had a grudge against Elise?" Tristan licked the end of his pen, which was already running out writing it all down at rapid pace.

"Oh gosh, *everyone* I should think. But not enough to kill her, well, except maybe Harvey and Kitty." Georgie lowered her voice dramatically. "I heard a story that Kitty and Harvey met first, and then Elise swooped in and stole him away just out of spite. I think Harvey always regretted his choice and knows he made the wrong one, but it was too late, he'd married the evil witch. I expect there's a prenup that stops him from ever marrying Kitty if he divorces Elise. I don't know how she'd wangle it, but that's the kind of thing she would do. Of course, it's probably different now she's dead, so there's your motive. She has an ex-husband too and you won't believe how she destroyed his life. There was this one time that…"

"Thank you, you've been extremely helpful." Tristan attempted to stem the flow of her gossip.

He faked mopping his brow once Georgie was gone. "She's a dynamo, isn't she?"

"I'm sure she'd leave you tired but happy," Morgana said, waspishly. "Let me guess, we have to talk to Keefe now? Do you really think he had someone in his room too?"

"Undoubtedly, and he won't kiss and tell either," Tristan replied, with good-natured annoyance. "Any thoughts about the mega-star before we talk to him?"

"He's shy," she told him, enjoying the look of surprise on Tristan's face. "At first I thought he was just aloof, or arrogant, or maybe even deadly dull, but actually, in hindsight, I don't think he's any of those things. My guess is that he wasn't prepared to be quite as famous as he's become, especially as it happened later in life, and he doesn't enjoy the spotlight."

"Strange choice of profession for someone who doesn't want to be in the spotlight," Tristan commented.

"Not really. After all, acting is about stepping out of yourself and being someone else. In a way, it's a perfect choice for shy people, so long as they can pull it off. They don't even have to think of what to say, they can just read the lines they're given."

"So, the man behind the myth is not that scary?"

"When have you ever been scared of anyone?" Morgana gave him a disbelieving look.

"It's pretty terrifying knowing that you can read every emotion I have." Tristan gave her a side glance.

Morgana felt her face go warm, knowing that she'd

intuited more than he probably wanted to reveal, but he'd never tried to hide it from her, he'd simply accepted that she would see it.

"Right, let's get this over with," Tristan said, "and maybe, just maybe, we might actually get some answers this time."

Chapter Fourteen

Keefe Mohan came into the library looking moody. He took a packet of cigarettes out of his pocket as he sat down, then looked around and clearly thought the better of it, replacing them again.

"I really don't think I can be of any help, I had very little to do with Elise Everett," he said, his voice deep and smooth.

Morgana tried not to feel overpowered by his velvety tone and to focus on seeing his aura as Tristan spoke. "I'm afraid we have a witness who overheard Mrs Everett threatening you last night. Something about going to the press with information about you?"

"Who told you that?" Keefe looked furious, and Morgana watched intently as all sorts of colours danced through his aura. It was interesting, there was definitely anger, but his fear was much stronger.

Whatever he's done, he's scared of us knowing, and yet he shows no shame or remorse. That could fit with murder? Though, shouldn't there be some *feelings of guilt?* Morgana thought, trying to read all the different colours. *And his anger is cold, not red hot like someone who'd commit a murder in a fit of rage.*

"I'm afraid we can't reveal that," Tristan was saying, apologetically. "But it would help enormously if you could simply tell us what happened between the two of you. At the moment the only information we have is that there was possibly someone else in your room, and Elise discovered this and was going to reveal it. You were heard saying that you would speak to her later, which suggests you may very well have been the person who went to her room and murdered her."

"I did not!" Keefe's face tightened further.

"I'm sure you didn't," Tristan said, calmly, "I'm just telling you how it might appear, and that you could easily clear it up for us if you would be willing?"

Keefe stared moodily at the books on the wall behind Tristan and Morgana and they waited in silence knowing that he was debating what to share.

"Very well," he said at last. "I have no idea why she came to my room last night. She has no interest in me, and I have none in her. But I know she likes to twist the knife, to manipulate others, just as Mrs Gossard does too. They are birds of a feather those two. I wish I had not come, I had no intention of doing so, but Mrs Gossard, she forced my hand. There is much she will do for her husband, things no one with any decency would consider. But Elise, she's only doing it for herself, she wants to hurt her husband not help him. I think that is why she was so angry at my rejection, she meant to betray him out of jealousy. But if she thought to destroy me then she underestimated me! I vowed I would take away her power!" The words spilled out of Keefe like a tirade.

Morgana blinked while trying to untangle so much information coupled with such a spiking of many different emotions.

Tristan didn't take his eyes off Keefe either, and wrote nothing down as he stared intently at the man. "What did you do?" Tristan asked, his tone sympathetic.

Morgana saw Tristan's own aura glow with alertness and knew he was expecting some kind of confession.

"I accepted myself! I will tell the world before she

can, I will not hide in the shadows any longer. I was with a man and not a woman. There! Now, none of them can control me, not Elise, not Judy Gossard either." Keefe sat back in the chair expelling a huge breath as though he'd been holding it for too long.

Tristan was quiet, clearly shifting his thoughts around, but Morgana couldn't contain all the questions buzzing in her brain from the different angles he'd revealed.

"Was Judy Gossard blackmailing you?" She asked.

Keefe nodded. "Not for money, she needs none. She just wants us all to be puppets on her string, she made me come here because it is what Bernie wanted. She controlled Elise too, and probably everyone else. But she didn't get to Dickie Magnus, he called me yesterday and told me that he was leaving his wife. Judy knew his secrets, but he'd had enough of her games. I thought he was crazy, his wife will take everything he cares about, but I understand now, she can't take his freedom." Keefe's voice had returned to his trademark velvet delivery, and Morgana got the feeling he was delivering lines that he'd played out in his head. But that didn't make them any less impactive and she was quite sure he was telling the truth.

She gave Tristan a small nod, and he nodded back, obviously in agreement.

Tristan finally opened his notebook and wrote a few lines, before saying, "Did you see where Elise went after she left you?"

"Straight to Judy, of course. I heard both their voices through my door."

"Are you quite sure it was Judy Gossard that you

heard speaking?"

"Yes, I was surprised because she takes the same sleeping pills that I do, Amoxin, they knock you out in minutes and it would take a great deal to rouse you. It's very taxing travelling all over and sleeping in different places. But I noticed that she sounded wide awake." Keefe seemed more relaxed now, as though a weight had been lifted from his shoulders. "You know, if I had to put money on who murdered Elise, then I'd have picked Judy over Harvey. She's got what it takes. But, I am biased against her."

"Thank you for your candour." Tristan favoured Keefe with a genuine smile of gratitude. "We appreciate *someone* at least being open."

"I don't want to have any secrets, not anymore." Keefe said, getting to his feet. "But I'd still ask that you kept my love life private, at least until I've had time to organise a proper press release."

"Of course, I don't see that it is relevant to the case," Tristan reassured Keefe.

Morgana squeezed her eyes shut the moment he was gone and pressed her palms against them.

"You're getting over-tired," Tristan said, sounding worried. "Would you rather I finished the interviews without you? You've done more than enough."

"No, I'm okay. It's just very mentally taxing. We might have to take another break before we continue."

"A stroll around the house together?" He suggested, taking her hands and pulling her to her feet. "I want to get a clearer idea of the layout. It seems like everyone has a room next to someone else, who may or may not have been spotted by them."

"It is a bit like that. The bedrooms go around a galley, so you can see side to side and across. I think Ethan is the only one around a corner." She wriggled a foot to dispel a sudden cramp.

"Oh yes, you took note of where he was, did you?" Tristan quirked his brows playfully, and she elbowed him as they made their way out to the Drawing Room.

Together they climbed the stairs in the main hall and Morgana pointed out the bedrooms she knew. Tristan walked around the gallery and back, coming to stop outside Elise's door.

"Let me see if I've got this right," he said. "First, you saw Georgiana Grace, going somewhere, then Lord Latheborne and Ethan Cope coming up to bed."

"Yes." Morgana agreed. "Though thinking about it, Bernie should have been with them, but wasn't."

"But he must have come upstairs, because he saw Elise going to Ethan's room, about an hour later?"

"Right. Then Ethan saw Georgie coming up the stairs almost straight after."

Morgana's eyes widened as she figured it out and Tristan smiled, coming to the same conclusion. "Bernie and Georgie," he confirmed.

Morgana pulled a face. "Not quite what I expected from her."

Tristan shrugged. "It's not that surprising though, he's still attractive, and powerful enough to help her a great deal."

"That's the bit that doesn't sit well. I thought women were pushing past the whole 'casting couch' expectations."

"Maybe she genuinely really likes him? They have a

lot in common and he's not *that* much older than her."

"But he is married."

"Regardless, the timing makes sense."

"Fine. Then Georgie sees Elise go to Keefe's room." She pointed down the corridor.

"Why didn't Elise see Georgie?" Tristan said, eyeing the angles.

"Because of the power cut. Most of the house was in total darkness. Only people actually moving about would be spotted in the candlelight."

He nodded and looked at his notebook. "Keefe has someone in his room, he sends Elise away, and she goes to Judy instead."

"Which means that, so far as we know, Judy was the last person to see her alive," Morgana surmised.

"Which also means we still have to interview Judy. Do you think she's as bad as she's painted?" Tristan gave her a quizzical look.

Morgana sighed. "I suspect she's even worse. I guessed that she was intuitive about others when I first met her, but she easily fooled me into thinking she was quite nice. She has a sense of humour which I appreciated. It wasn't until she made it clear that she knew I wasn't Morwenna, and that she would be holding onto that information for her own purposes, that I started to realise there was more to her than she let on."

"Hmm, it will be interesting to meet her," Tristan said, leading the way back downstairs. "I'm going to go and call DI Lowen and let him know what we've discovered so far, which means I'll have to walk to the end of the driveway. Will you join me back in the library in about half an hour?"

"Yes, of course." Morgana waited until he was out the door then went back to her own bedroom to see if she could find an aspirin or at least some water to try to ease the headache that was beginning to form behind her eyes.

Twenty minutes later she went back downstairs, but as expected, there was no sign of Tristan yet, so instead, she began to poke her head through all the doors to rooms she had yet to explore. She located the Billiard Room and found that it did indeed have big wide cushioned seats around three of the walls, which would make it a good place for a cosy chat. She also discovered a study that was clearly designed for the lady of the house. It was well dusted, but the sense of disuse was obvious.

"Needs a woman in it," she commented to herself, running her hand over the smooth walnut top of the desk.

"It does, doesn't it?"

She turned quickly and found Ethan leaning against the frame of the door.

"Oh, hi. You startled me. I was just exploring." She gave him a smile, but he didn't return it.

"Finally alone," he said, holding out his arms. "Come here."

"Urm," she mumbled, unsure what to do. "I'm just admiring this desk."

"See yourself sitting there? Is that it?" He dropped his arms.

"What?"

"Is there something going on between you and my uncle?" He came straight to the point.

She frowned. "Of course not. Why on earth would you think that?"

"I don't know. A vibe, I suppose? You're being different with me, distant. I've been trying to work out why."

"It's a bit of a leap from me being different, to me having a secret affair with your uncle." She knew she was hedging, but she didn't really know what else to say to keep from revealing that she wasn't who he thought she was.

"I'm not stupid, Morwenna. I can pick up on the undercurrents."

"The undercurrents? What undercurrents?" She stared at him, genuinely confused.

"Are you saying they're not there?" He took a step toward her. "I need you to tell me the truth because right now I'm imagining all sorts and it feels pretty crappy."

His expression changed, reminding her again that he wasn't as old as he pretended to be. She could see his vulnerability and as he took another step toward her she realised that he was expecting some sort of reassurance. In fact, she had the notion that she was about to get kissed for the second time that day.

Months of nothing and then all the trains come in at once? She thought, feeling like it was just her kind of luck.

She took a hasty step back and he looked hurt.

She cursed her sister again in her mind and knew he deserved better than she was giving him. "Ethan, I'm not who you think I am."

"Are any of us?" He stepped closer again. "I know you're not always going to be a party girl, I know you're a genuine person underneath all the fun times we've had.

That's okay with me, I can do sincere as well." He put his arms around her.

"That's not what I meant," she said, trying to wriggle free. "I'm not Morwenna. I'm really sorry I deceived you, but we've never actually met before this weekend. So, I'm not deliberately snubbing you, I just don't know you!"

His grip loosened, his face filled with suspicion. "I see. You have dual personality disorder?" His tone was heavy with sarcasm now.

She sighed, ducking under his arm and away from him. "Did Morwenna ever tell you she had a twin sister?"

"No."

"Oh. Well, she does. That would be me."

"I don't believe you." He was looking at her with dislike now, clearly feeling he was being meanly brushed off.

Morgana clenched her jaw, trying to keep her temper in check. "You know her pretty well, right? Like intimately well?"

"I know *you* that well, yes."

"Have you ever seen any of her tattoos?"

His eyes went to her shoulder and she knew that he had.

"Then look." Morgana pulled her top away from her shoulder, showing bare skin and a bra strap. "Did it magically vanish?"

He stared at her shoulder and Morgana held her ground as he reached out to touch the place where Morwenna was inked but she wasn't. He ran his thumb over the skin.

"Huh," he said finally, looking amazed. His eyes returned to her face. "But why?"

"It's a long story. But basically, I'm here as a favour to her, and you weren't supposed to be here. No one else knows I'm not her. Except the police, of course." She didn't feel the need to explain that Judy knew, as she couldn't see how it made any difference.

"You didn't tell my uncle? You should, you know, he values honesty."

"What he values isn't really relevant right now. This was a favour for Morwenna, and now it's a murder investigation. The fact that your uncle doesn't like me isn't top of my priority list." Morgana checked her watch and made to leave the room. It was time to meet Tristan.

Ethan gave her a calculating look and then stepped out of her way. But his voice followed her. "You really should tell him."

Chapter Fifteen

"Hey," Tristan greeted when she returned to the library. "Been up to any sleuthing?"

"Not really, just clearing up a misunderstanding." She gave a small smile and plonked down into her chair.

"Well, I've found out a few things from my DI. We've had the preliminary autopsy back."

"Oh yes?" He had her full attention now.

"Elise Everett definitely died from being stabbed repeatedly, but she wouldn't have known about it. She was full of Amoxin, at least four times a normal dose."

"Amoxin? Isn't that the sleeping drug that Keefe said he takes?" Morgana screwed up her face, sure that someone else in the house also took the same thing.

"Yes, and Judy, according to Keefe, remember?"

"That's not it." She tapped her lip, trying to recall. "I know, Georgie told me that Elise *takes enough tranks to knock an elephant out.* So, she could have dosed herself?"

Tristan held up a hand and flicked through his notes. "You're right. Here it is. The maid, Bonny. She said she went in early by mistake, then saw that Mr. Everett wasn't there and that Mrs. Everett hadn't taken her pills. Which is a funny thing to notice, don't you think?"

"Not if she really was there to steal the jewellery. She'd expect her mistress to be out for the count, and she probably knew perfectly well that Harvey would sneak to Kitty's room. Servants always know that kind of stuff. So, she noticed that the pills weren't taken before she even noticed the blood?" Morgana speculated.

"Makes sense." Tristan made a scribble in the margin of the page. "But why was she stealing the jewellery here and now, why not any other night?"

Morgana shrugged. "Plenty of suspects? Or maybe they are usually kept in a safe. They would be if Elise was at home or staying at a hotel. But here there was no option but to keep them out?"

"Regardless. If Bonny is correct then Elise didn't actually take her pills. So, did someone else give them to her? We need to find out exactly who takes Amoxin and if they have any missing. It's a prescription-only drug, so we can probably trace that." He pulled out his phone and briefly asked Constable Dunn to find out exactly who in the household had Amoxin.

"Any other news?"

"Yes. Harvey was sure that Elise had taken her pills as normal and so he snuck out to see Kitty at about eleven pm. It's possible that she simply faked doing so. They both claim they hadn't left her bedroom at all until Bonny started screaming."

"That could be quite true. Georgie came to my room at about eleven and said there was someone sneaking about, so it was probably Harvey?"

"Harvey also confirmed that all Elise's jewellery was accounted for, but we did find some blood on the pearls. He also says that several pieces have gone missing in the past. So, I think Lord Latheborne's guess about Bonny was probably correct too. I suspect she had actually lifted them, but then saw the body and decided it would be smart to put them back."

"Or, maybe she got caught this time and had to resort to murder?" Morgana suggested.

"Except that we know Elise was drugged unconscious before then. The Amoxin was mixed in with some hot cocoa, and it seems likely that Bonny would have been the one to give it to her, but that would concur more with the idea that she was making sure her mistress was asleep when she robbed her. However, I've just been to the kitchen to ask Bonny if she gave her any cocoa and she swears she didn't. None of the staff have any recollection of Elise ordering or making hot cocoa last night." Tristan frowned and tapped his pen on his book.

"Maybe Judy gave it to her?"

"Yes," he agreed. "That's exactly what I was thinking. Are you mentally ready to deal with her?"

Morgana nodded and then closed her eyes, opening up her other senses in preparation. "Bring on the queen bee," she said. But she wasn't nearly as prepared as she thought, because when Judy entered the room, she surprised Morgana. Her aura was blue. Pure aqua.

Oh crap, Morgana thought, eyeing Judy with trepidation. *This woman doesn't lie. Which means that she's too smart to be seen through. She's going to outwit us without giving away a thing.*

Tristan, however, couldn't see Judy's aura, and Morgana couldn't really tell him, so instead, she had to wait while he posed the question about Elise.

"Yes, I saw her last night. I was probably the last person to see her alive, apart from her killer of course," Judy said, still radiating honesty. "She was in a terrible temper, she wanted revenge on her husband, revenge on her sister, by the time I saw her, she wanted revenge on half the house. She needed to be loved and adored, you see. She needed to be number one."

"What did she say to you?" Tristan asked.

"Oh, nothing of interest. Just a lot of hot air about what she was going to do to them all. That's what she does, she sticks the knife in and then she twists it." Judy was quite blithe as she said it.

"Rather an apt expression seeing as she was stabbed," Tristan commented.

"Yes, which rather give the impression that the killer was taking an act of personal revenge doesn't it?" Judy smiled broadly.

"It does," agreed Tristan. "Do you have any idea what that revenge might have been?"

Judy waved an airy hand. "Well, Elise has done so many terrible things to people. Do you know she once pushed a woman off a balcony at a party? Broke her back. A sweet young actress named Sarah Finch. The poor girl ended up in a wheelchair. The doctors said she'd never walk again."

"Elise did that? But why?" Morgana was horrified. "Shouldn't she have at least been charged with grievous bodily harm?"

"The girl was up and coming and she beat Elise to a role. But there was no proof it was Elise who pushed her. Just one word against another. And then a witness came forward who claimed that Elise was out in the garden with him when it happened and that was the end of it. Funnily enough, the witness was a stunt man who'd had an affair with Elise, and shortly after that he retired from the business and started his own company. Doing scuba tours on a Greek Island, I think. He somehow managed to buy the entire island." Judy raised her brows at Morgana, as if telling her to read something into her words.

"You're suggesting Elise paid him off?"

"That would be my guess. It was unfortunate that he was eaten by a shark six months later, or so they say." Again there was insinuation in her tone.

"Mrs. Gossard," Tristan said assertively, trying to bring her back to the topic in question. "Do you know what Elise did after you saw her?"

"Of course, dear. I know what everyone in this house was doing. Elise was all worked up, and I told her to order herself some warm milk and go back to bed. There was nothing to be gained by trying to get one up on her husband, he was a lost cause. He didn't love her anymore, you see. It was just a matter of time before he left her. Sometimes husbands just need to stretch their legs a little, feel virile still, but Harvey wasn't like that. He was just working up the nerve to act, he knew what she really was." Judy nodded sagely to herself.

"He was scared of her?" Tristan asked.

"Undoubtedly." Judy smiled. "She wasn't a very nice woman. But then, women seldom are. Oh, don't look so miffed, Morgana dear. You aren't exactly *holier than thou* yourself this weekend."

Morgana clenched her teeth and tried not to let Judy get under her skin as the other woman clearly intended to do. "You say you know what everyone in the house was doing? Could you elaborate?"

"I could…" Judy pursed her lips, as though considering it. "Keefe Mohan was having illicit relations with the butler in his bedroom. But I suspect you've already worked that one out. Georgie was seducing my husband downstairs, but that didn't take long. Poor Bernie doesn't have a great deal of stamina. She was in her own bed alone when the murder happened, and Bernie will have spent most of the night doodling on the script. He doesn't sleep much, not even after sewing his few remaining oats. And you, Morgana, you were hiding in your room from both Ethan Cope and Lord Latheborne, while they had to sleep alone in theirs. No, no, don't deny it, I know you were tempted, but it was tricky wasn't it, pretending to be someone else?" She wagged an admonishing finger at Morgana who bit her inner cheek hard to stop herself from giving Judy the satisfaction of getting a reaction.

"Which just leaves you, free to commit murder," Morgana ground out, earning herself a reproving look from Tristan.

"Except it wasn't me," Judy said, still smiling in a way that Morgana found extremely patronising.

"Have you any idea who it might be?" Tristan broke in, clearly seeing the metaphorical steam coming from Morgana's ears.

Judy wagged her finger again, this time at him. "That's your job, not mine. I might know many secrets, but they are my stock in trade."

Morgana focussed hard on Judy's aura, which hadn't changed colour at all throughout the interview. "Do you think Harvey might have killed his wife?" She asked a direct question instead of an open one, trying to elicit a different reaction.

"I think it was far more likely that she'd murder him first. She told me she wanted to poison him like the rat he was. Yes, she was very angry last night," Judy said, still managing to avoid any answer that might show as a lie. Her aura remained as blue as a midday sea.

"Did you know that she didn't take her sleeping pills, despite giving Harvey the impression that she had?" he persisted.

"Obviously."

"The same pills that you take, I believe?"

Judy tilted her head. "Is that an insinuation, Detective Sergeant? I had precisely twenty Amoxin when we arrived here, which you can probably verify with your airport in London, seeing as they made a note of it. I still have twenty. Maybe it's the country air, but I feel terribly well rested in this house." She looked smug again, as though something else had given her the relaxation she needed. If Morgana had to guess then she'd say that Judy had been enjoying herself, murder and all. Information was her opiate.

"You know who it was, don't you?" Morgana accused, heightening her senses in readiness to open her third eye.

"No." Judy's aura abruptly changed colour, from blue to yellow. The colour looked very wrong on her, and Morgana could tell it was a rare sight.

"She's lying," Morgana said, looking directly at Tristan and willing him to force the truth out of Judy.

But Tristan merely held up a hand to quiet Morgana.

"Withholding information is not only illegal, but also dangerous," he kept his voice soft and his attention on Judy.

"If that's all, DS Treharne, then I'm awfully thirsty and I believe it's nearly time for an afternoon tiffin." Judy glanced at her watch. "I do so love the English custom of day time drinking. It's a total faux pas in L.A. but here, it's almost *de rigueur*."

"How could you let her walk away without telling us everything?" Morgana almost ground out at Tristan as soon as Judy was gone.

"Because she wasn't going to tell us, it's as simple as that." He replied evenly. "You see emotions, Morgana, but I see people, and I know when to push them and when it's a waste of time to try."

Morgana stared up at the ceiling as if seeking divine inspiration to calm down. "What now?" she asked when she had expended the last of her exasperation on a few huffed out breaths.

"I'm not sure. I should get back to the station and cross-check my notes with that of DI Lowen. He'll want to go through everything I've found out. I suppose we'll return tomorrow with a whole new set of questions."

They left the library and found Keefe and Georgie waiting in the hall, both with luggage at their feet.

"You're leaving?" Morgana asked, surprised that she hadn't even considered that they would.

"We can't stay here, we've been talking and we're not at all convinced that Harvey and Kitty murdered Elise. Which means there could still be a killer in the house!" Georgie stated.

"I'm afraid you can't leave the area, we're not done with our inquiry," Tristan said, sternly.

"I have a plane ticket booked for tomorrow night." Keefe angled his chin at Tristan dismissively. "I have commitments elsewhere, it is not possible to stay."

Bernie came into the hall at that moment and took up a stance blocking the front door. "Now, see here. You don't have anywhere you have to be, you're committed to me first and foremost. This weekend gathering is scheduled until after lunch tomorrow, and not one of you has any place to be other than here until then! We've had this in your diaries for nearly a year now, so don't you even think of bailing on me."

Tristan frowned at Keefe and Georgie. "You can't leave the country, not until we've determined who committed the crime."

There was a babble of noise as Keefe and Georgie both protested loudly.

"Fine, but you can't make us stay in this house." Georgie stamped her foot.

"You're under contract to do just that," Bernie insisted loudly. "What you do *after* that is your own business, fly to Timbuktu for all I care."

Morgana stepped forward and put a hand on Georgie's as she reached for her suitcase. "Why not stay just until tomorrow? Then you can leave after lunch as planned and no one has broken any contracts? I'm sure the police could leave someone here as a guard if you feel unsafe."

"In your bedroom perhaps?" Georgie sniffed contemptuously.

"Miss Emrys, a word please?" Tristan barked at Morgana and she stepped away from the others unwillingly.

"What? You can leave someone here, can't you?"

"It's not that. The problem is that if they all leave tomorrow then we'll have one hell of a job keeping them all in the U.K. These people fly all over the world at the drop of a hat, and we're going to have to start confiscating passports if we haven't solved this by lunchtime!"

"Then we'll have to make sure we do." Morgana patted his arm. "I have faith in you DS Treharne."

"I can't stay here, Morgana. I need to go over the statements and work out the timeline of events. I can leave Poppy or Cartwright, and I'll be back first thing, but are you sure you feel safe? Maybe it's for the best if they do leave and find alternative local accommodation."

Morgana shook her head. "The best chance we have is to keep them all here together, then watch and listen. Don't you usually pick up clues when people let their guard down? I can keep them talking, over dinner and breakfast, see if anyone reveals anything."

Tristan gave her an indulgent smile. "No, that's not really how I 'pick up clues', I rely on facts and evidence, but I agree that it's how *you* work best, and as we're on a clock right now I'm prepared to take all the help you can give. You're my eyes and ears here, okay? Just be careful, promise me?"

"Why, Tristan. One might almost think you cared," she replied flippantly, slightly unsettled by his worried expression.

"You already know I do." He turned away and addressed the group in the hall. "I'm going to leave a constable here tonight. I can't force you to stay, but we'd prefer it if you did. Your cooperation in our investigation is much appreciated." And with that, he set off up the stairs to locate his constables.

Chapter Sixteen

Feeling tired of keeping her senses up, and despite the fact that she'd now dampened them back down, Morgana chose to avoid the others as they gathered in the drawing-room for afternoon tea or afternoon cocktails in the case of some. Instead, she widened her wandering and explored more of the house. She went past all the bedrooms and along the corridor toward the rear of the house where she found the entrance to the gothic tower she'd noticed on her arrival. She curiously ascended the steps, passing a door halfway up, but kept going to the room at the top. It had at some point been a bedroom, but now housed nothing but trunks and dusty boxes. She resisted the urge to search through them and instead went to the window to check out the view.

The moor stretched out for miles behind the house. Lonely, windswept, and stunningly beautiful in her opinion. She opened the catch on the arched frame and felt distinctly like Rapunzel as she leaned out.

From the window beneath her came the sound of music and she pulled her head in again. She relatched the window and went back down, pausing as she reached the landing and the door she'd passed on her way up. She couldn't hear the music now.

Strange, maybe another ghost? She thought.

She turned the handle on the door and it swung open. The music immediately greeted her and she realised that the room must be soundproofed.

You wouldn't want to get trapped in here with a murderer! She shivered as the notion crossed her mind. But taking a tentative step inside she saw Lord Latheborne seated at a piano by the window, staring out as he played. The top portion of the window was ajar despite the chill outside, and as she watched a small, scruffy, black and white cat squeezed its body in through the gap and leapt down, landing on the baby grand.

"Hey, Mozart." Lord Latheborne stopped playing and reached out a hand to scratch the top of the cat's head.

The cat allowed it for a second then turned to stare balefully at Morgana. Lord Latheborne turned his head to see what the cat was looking at and gave her almost the exact same look.

She couldn't help but smile. "Sorry, am I intruding?"

"Of course not," he said, though his tone suggested otherwise.

"I didn't know you had a cat." She suddenly liked him much better than she had.

"I don't, not really, he's a stray. It's taken me months to get him to trust me, but he's still skittish."

"And you call him Mozart?" Morgana reached out and let the little cat sniff her fingertips. She also used just a hint of magic to project safety and reassurance to the animal. Mozart responded immediately by relaxing and rolling onto his back so that Morgana could rub his tummy.

"He likes the music, he comes when I play, and seems to favour Mozart." Lord Latheborne gave an almost embarrassed laugh.

"He's a she," Morgana informed him, feeling the lumps on the cat's tummy, "and pregnant, if I'm not mistaken."

"You're kidding. Oh no!" He glared at the cat,

before reaching out to pet her again. "You realise what this means, Mozart? It means you're going to have to start eating properly!"

Morgana warmed to him even more at this announcement. "I think she's ready to be persuaded."

He shook his head. "She won't go anywhere else inside the house, only in this one room. I suppose I could arrange to have some food put out here."

"She's wary, but she trusts you. Some food in here is a great idea, and a bed too, an old box with a blanket if you can spare one. But she'll venture out further now she's chosen you to be the kitten daddy." Morgana made a kissy noise at the cat and Mozart jumped from the piano and up onto her shoulder, pressing her face against Morgana's and purring.

"Good grief." Lord Latheborne blinked in surprise. "How did you get her to do that? She won't usually go near anyone but me."

"I have a way with cats, comes with the territory." She spoke without really thinking, alluding to her witchy heritage, but thankfully he didn't pick up on it.

"Wait, what do you mean *kitten daddy*?"

"I mean that she'll have them here, probably right in this room. Cats naturally seek out a safe space and quite often a person to provide for them when pregnant. And as yours is the only house for miles…Well, it's you."

"Marvellous," he said sarcastically, but his eyes softened on the cat and he scratched her head again. Mozart jumped off Morgana's shoulder and seated herself back on the piano, staring at the keys almost expectantly.

They both laughed.

"I guess she wants you to keep playing. I'll leave you to it." Morgana backed from the room and quietly closed the door, aware that her mood had greatly improved during the last few minutes.

She went to her own bedroom and then to the bathroom, and was feeling back at full strength when she finally went downstairs all spruced and dressed for pre-dinner drinks.

The mood was instantly altered when she spotted Poppy Dunn, in police uniform, standing at the bottom of the stairs. Her presence a sharp reminder to Morgana that she was about mingle with the other guests and that one of them was possibly a knife-wielding murderer.

Chapter Seventeen

The scene in the drawing-room looked very much like the evening before to Morgana. Adams was mixing drinks and everyone was dressed up. She cast a regretful glance over her shoulder at Poppy, thinking how much she'd prefer being in the Portmage pub with her rather than drinking cocktails with this lot. But she squared her shoulders, slapped on a smile, and sallied forth. *Once more unto the breach,* she quoted silently. But this time without the benefit of being able to see their mood. Her magical muscle was utterly exhausted from overuse earlier in the day, and she had been very relieved to tamp it down for a rest. Probably just in time before she got a migraine.

"So, you decided to stay?" Morgana made straight for Georgie, who was just downing a very large cocktail.

"Bernie said he'd cast someone else if I didn't." Georgie pulled a face. "I can't imagine why he's so keen for us all to remain here for the night. It's not as though we've got a great deal done, is it?"

"On the other hand, it's definitely been the bonding experience he hoped for." Morgana looked at Keefe who was smiling and chatting to Ethan, and looked happier than she'd seen him since he'd arrived. Judy was also on good form and was drawing Lord Latheborne out on his family history, while Bernie was having a go at charming Constable Dunn, trying and succeeding in persuading her to join them in the room.

"So, you and Bernie don't have an *on-going* understanding?" Morgana asked, lowering her voice.

Georgie grinned over the edge of her cocktail glass. "Worked it out, did you? And no, we don't. He was just cutting loose a little, and I have a weakness for powerful men, don't you think there's something about them?"

Morgana thought of her recent boyfriends, among them were a gardener and a chef, hardly powerful in the way Georgie meant it. "Not really, no."

"That's not what I read, Morwenna," Georgie teased, instantly reminding Morgana that she was supposed to be someone rather different from herself. "Still, I do like your type too. That policeman was divine. Sort of cold but hot, a tantalising combination."

"But nothing at all like Bernie," Morgana pointed out.

"No." Georgie glanced over to where Bernie was standing. "I know it doesn't make sense, but the truth is that he and I have a great deal in common. We both come from very poor backgrounds, in fact, we even grew up in the same rough neighbourhood, though a couple of decades apart. His wife comes from privilege, she'll never really get him like I do. We found a common ground straight away, faking it with the high flyers. What's the saying? Fake *it until you make it.* I guess we've both made it now, but you still never really feel like you fit. We don't need to pretend around each other."

Despite not having her senses open, Morgana saw a visible flare of pink emanate from Georgie and realised that the other woman was in love. "It sounds to me like you care a great deal for him?" she asked softly.

Georgie necked the rest of her drink. "He'll never leave his wife, she's too useful to him." A fleeting look of sadness passed over her face and Morgana noticed that Georgie didn't even try to deny her feelings.

"Well, I'm going to get another loaded martini and

flirt with Keefe, wish me luck!" Georgie reverted to her wide smile.

"Good luck," Morgana said with amusement, looking over at Keefe, who still talking but whose eyes were following Adams as he circled the room with canapés.

As soon as Georgie had left her side, Judy sidled over.

"I see Ethan has lost interest in you, I assume you told him the truth about who you really are?" she asked, with a sly knowing look upon her face.

"It occurs to me, Judy, that if you were to use your powers for good instead of evil then you'd make an excellent police detective," Morgana commented.

Judy laughed, clearly not offended in the slightest. "That would be less fun. Now, tell me some things about you, the real you. You're a bit of a mystery as you're giving a good performance of being someone else."

"Isn't everyone here giving a good performance? That's their meal ticket, right? And I'm including you," Morgana sniped, not willing to give Judy an ounce of grist for her mill.

"Very astute, my dear. To most, I'm just the wife, but I suppose most people do acknowledge that behind every great man…You, however, saw straight through it, didn't you? Yes, I like you." Judy looked at her approvingly and Morgana felt uncomfortable, like a butterfly trapped by a collector.

A shiver of apprehension went through her and it suddenly crossed her mind that Judy was the perfect murderer. Who would suspect her? And yet, those who knew her, like Georgie and Keefe, had both suggested that she was manipulative. Of course, Georgie was biased, but Keefe had said that Judy was actually just like Elise. And even Elise had been under Judy's power.

Morgana took a step backward as the feeling of darkness around Judy seemed to intensify.

"What are you thinking?" Morgana couldn't help but ask. Something had to be creating that tangible tang of foreboding that she could sense.

"I'm thinking about what kind of a person it takes to commit a murder. Not just anyone could do it. The physical act is easy of course, any thug can pull a trigger, and even the most innocent-seeming could administer poison. But the emotional and mental strength it requires, you have to respect that, don't you?"

Morgana stared at her, putting some pieces together. Judy had been the last person to see Elise alive. Judy took Amoxin and maybe had an extra stash concealed somewhere. Judy was the one who suggested the hot chocolate. Judy had probably been alone when Elise was murdered. Why had Elise gone to Judy? To free herself, just as Keefe intended to do? How would Judy have taken that?

"Excuse me, I just need to have a word with Constable Dunn." Morgana moved away from Judy and made eye contact with Poppy.

Poppy saw Morgana's face and quickly detached herself from Bernie, meeting her halfway by the window. "Everything okay, Morgana?"

Morgana's mouth tilted. "You realised it's me?"

"I'd like to say yes, but actually Tristan told me. I know not to say anything though." Poppy leaned in close. "You have that look on your face like you've sensed something?"

"You're right. I'm thinking that Judy has all the hallmarks of being the murderer."

"Judy Gossard?" Poppy was surprised but smart enough not to show it on her face or to look over at Judy. "Are you sure? She seems very sweet."

"She's not," Morgana assured her.

"Got it. I'll keep an eye on her. I'll be stationing myself right in the front hall for the night, so I don't think people will be attempting all the liaisons and wandering again this evening."

"Morwenna, darling?" Ethan broke into their conversation, his eyes dancing with humour at sharing the secret of her true identity. "Would you care you stroll on the patio with me?"

"In the dark, and cold?" Morgana gave him a narrow look. "And how do I know you're not the murderer luring me away from the others?"

"Do you think I have a murderous quality about me? I'll take that as a compliment." Ethan beamed at her. "But actually I wanted to go for a cigarette and hardly anyone here smokes. It's so millennial of them."

Morgana rolled her eyes and gestured to the French Doors that were hidden behind some heavy velvet curtains. "Fine, I'll come and watch you kill yourself slowly with tobacco. Better than being stabbed, I suppose."

"Damn, that means you trust me. I guess I don't have the range to play a serial killer after all."

"Nobody said serial killer," Morgana pointed out as they stepped outside and the cold air immediately made it's presence felt.

Ethan slipped off his evening jacket and draped it around her shoulders. Morgana generally considered herself a feminist and would have declined if he'd actually offered it, on the grounds that she didn't need it any more than he did, but the jacket felt too warm and silky to give up once it was on her, and she figured that her inner woman didn't like to suffer.

"Serial killers are much more fun as a role. Crimes of passion are personal, wouldn't you say? And have a limited storyline revolving around a single event in general, but to be a serial killer is more about the psychosis of the murderer and requires more depth. It's less about the victim and their story."

"You mean, you want to be the only lead character," Morgana responded. But Ethan's comments were making her think. The fact that Elise had been so brutally stabbed did suggest a very personal vendetta. And she was almost certain this had been very much about the victim and their story. Elise had been responsible for ruining a lot of people's lives. The question was, who had she hurt so badly that they'd want to see her dead and be mad enough to make it happen?

"Is seeing Morwenna the real reason you came here this weekend?" Morgana asked.

"Checking out my alibi?" Ethan leaned against the balustrade and lit his cigarette. "Not really, it's all one big networking gig, isn't it? Become more friendly with Bernie, charm his wife, meet Keefe Mohan. Sleeping with Morwenna was a side perk." He reached out and curled a lock of Morgana's hair around his finger. "You look so much like her, it's difficult to separate you in my head. But she has a fire in her that you don't."

Morgana jerked her hair away, feeling insulted.

"Sorry," he said, sounding genuine. "It's not a bad thing. You're more grounded, more grown-up. It's probably a good thing that you're here and not her. I imagine that whatever it is you do with the police, she couldn't?"

"That's true." Morgana was somewhat mollified. She'd always felt that her sister had more power than she did, as Morwenna could move energy with her mind. But while Morgana's power might be less physical, it was a darn sight more useful in cases like this. "I'm better at reading people than she is."

Ethan smiled. "What do you read in me? Am I actually a suspect?"

Morgana shook her head. "I don't think so. And you weren't supposed to be here anyway. Not that I suppose that matters. It could have been a spur of the moment murder."

"But assuming it wasn't, that means it was premeditated, right? Someone could have been plotting this for months and months. I mean, actors and directors and so on, they often book their diaries years in advance. This weekend was planned months ago, so it wouldn't take much for someone to create an alibi or get themselves a place on this jaunt if they were looking for a chance to take out Elise. It's quite a good spot to do it, the local cops won't be half as thorough as The Met, or the LAPD."

"Yes, they will." Morgana felt defensive on behalf of Tristan and the others.

"Well, let's hope so. They've basically got until tomorrow lunchtime to solve it before everyone scarpers, and then they'll have a high old time trying to keep track of them."

Morgana drummed her fingernails on the stonework, acknowledging that this was true. It was exactly what Tristan had said too. She needed to somehow step up the investigation because the clock was ticking on being able to question everyone. So far, she and Tristan had covered most of the household, but not everyone.

Judy was still her prime suspect, but she didn't have any evidence. She could hardly go and start searching bedrooms, that was more the official side of things. No, she needed to get people talking and see if she could spot any obvious lies or inconsistencies.

"Do you take sleeping pills?" she asked Ethan, as casually as she could.

He laughed, obviously seeing straight through her words. "Of course not. That kind of trouble is usually for older people, isn't it? I find a good horizontal workout does the trick far better. Unfortunately, that option seems off the table for me this weekend. I can tell you're not into it, not with me anyway, and everyone else is practically decrepit. Even Georgie is clearly way older than she pretends. Louise has got herself a boyfriend and doesn't cheat, as she's already informed me in the strongest terms. Hey, do you think that pretty policewoman might be tempted?"

Morgana tutted at him, not only for his rampant lust but also because he'd just flicked his cigarette butt out into the garden with complete disregard for the wildlife. "I think Constable Dunn will absolutely *not* be seduced while on duty."

"I'll take that as a maybe." He gave a boyish grin. "I

think they want us to go back in, looks like everyone is going to get ready for dinner."

Morgana gave a resentful sigh. "I'd have thought we could dispense with all the old world charade in light of what's happened."

"Are you kidding?" He held the door open for her to go inside first. "That's what they live for; no pun intended."

Ethan was right, Morgana realised, as she came back downstairs almost an hour later and found everyone gussied up to the nines again. It was extremely fortunate that she'd added a little black dress as an afterthought, and though the poor thing had been rolled in a ball and wedged into her suitcase, it had the benefit of being crease-proof and had tumbled out looking none the worse.

She took in Georgie, radiant in another pink cocktail dress, and was relieved she hadn't needed to borrow anything from her. *I doubt that my hips would fit into a single thing she owns*, she thought ruefully.

Despite the murder hanging over them all, and the addition of a police officer in the house, the mood seemed light-hearted. Morgana supposed that the fact that none of them had liked Elise probably accounted for that, but it still seemed a bit too relaxed considering one of them might easily be the murderer!

The others seemed to be thinking along the same lines as her because in a quiet moment, as they all finished their soup, Georgie spoke up. "So, which was of us did her in? That's what I'm bursting with curiosity to know. Do we all accept it was Harvey and Kitty? Personally, I have my doubts."

There was a sudden cacophony around the table as people espoused various theories. But the one thing she picked up on loud and clear was that quite a lot of them also were of the mind that Harvey didn't have it in him.

"Kitty might have pushed him into it," Keefe suggested, "or done it herself. Don't underestimate a woman in love."

Morgana shook her head. "I don't think Kitty is the type either, plus she struck me as being fairly rational and intelligent. I think that if she was going to murder Elise then she wouldn't have done it in such an obvious way."

They all pondered on that for a moment as Mrs. Brown brought in a tray carrying a large pheasant and began to portion it out at the side table. Louise laid out bowls of peas, carrots, and potatoes, while Adams moved clockwise around the table topping up wine glasses.

"But a good actress can play the role of a decent person while secretly plotting," Judy put in, once she'd helped herself to some of everything. "It's not difficult to completely reinvent yourself and pretend to be someone else. Perhaps even acquiring a whole new name."

Morgana opened her mouth to try to shut Judy up, as the comment seemed to be directed straight at her, but she was saved from having to think of the right thing to say by a loud crashing of dishes behind her.

She turned and found Mrs. Brown, Louise, and Adams all looking horrified at an upturned plate of pheasant that had just hit the floor.

"Apologies, Sir." Adams gave a pained look at Lord Latheborne. "I thought I had it."

"No need, these things happen." Lord Latheborne gave them all a reassuring smile. Mrs. Brown had turned pale at the disaster and was on her hands and knees brushing the ruined food off the floor and into a large napkin, while Louise ran to the kitchen to fetch a cloth and another plate.

"Kitty wasn't an actress though, was she?" Lord Latheborne said, bringing them back on topic and diverted everyone's attention away from his staff.

"No, no talent for it at all," Bernie put in. "Elise once tried to get her a small part in a play she was in, but Kitty couldn't remember her lines and got terrible stage fright."

"Which fits with the personality we know her as," agreed Georgie. "Still, it was unusually kind of Elise to try to bring Kitty into the fold?"

"I think Elise enjoyed how much the whole thing pained Kitty. The poor girl spent years trying to get on with her sister, but Elise was a narcissist. They only see how things are for themselves and never appreciate others."

"Then aren't you fortunate to have me, dear," Judy sharply pointed out to her husband. "I spend most of my time doing things for you."

Morgana wanted to reply that she'd completely misinterpreted the principle of narcissism, but her attention was caught by Judy's words. Was she actually saying that she might have done something for him, something like murder? That could be a motive!

On the other hand, she decided not to rule out Bernie himself. If he had a reason for wanting Elise out of the way, then she felt he was capable of murder if pushed. Bernie hadn't wanted Elise for his lead role, she'd been pushed on him by Dickie Magnus. Or maybe he'd done it for love? Now that she knew he was involved with Georgie, it was possible he'd killed Elise to give his girlfriend the role he'd originally intended to be hers all along? It was a flimsy motive, but there could be plenty of other reasons she didn't know about.

She wished Poppy was in the room, but her friend was on duty and had stationed herself at a chair in the hall, refusing to join them for dinner.

"Adams?" Morgana said, wondering if Poppy was hungry. "Would you mind if I took an extra plate of food out to Constable Dunn?"

"It's been done, miss," Adams assured her. "She refused the pheasant, but eventually accepted a sandwich. I made sure to add a few extras to the tray." He winked at her and Morgana beamed back at him, grateful that he was so excellent at his job. She had no doubt that Poppy was enjoying far more than a mere sandwich.

"Would you mind giving me two desserts in that case? I bet I can persuade her to have some of that delicious-looking cake too."

Adams nodded, and ten minutes later Morgana was able to excuse herself from the table on the pretext of taking her friend some pudding, and went to share her suspicions with Poppy.

Chapter Eighteen

After chatting for a while with Poppy, Morgana decided she really couldn't face rejoining the rest of the party and instead headed up to her bedroom for some quiet time. But as she passed the door to Elise's bedroom she heard noises from within and paused to listen. Someone seemed to be sobbing and it sounded as though they were searching the room at the same time. Very quietly and slowly, Morgana reached out and turned the door handle. It was locked. She frowned over that. She remembered now that Lord Latheborne had locked the door and given the key to Tristan, so how had the person inside got in? There was no other door into the room, apart from the one leading to Bonny's room. But this too was inaccessible from anywhere else. It was just a small chamber and would probably once have been a ladies' dressing room.

Could someone have climbed in a window? There was a parapet running along the upper floor level outside, so she supposed it was technically possible. But who? The sobs definitely sounded like a woman.

Morgana went down on one knee to peer through the keyhole and immediately caught a glimpse of a person pacing the floor. Or, rather, a former person. A ghost, to be precise.

Oh great, just what this house needs, yet another ghost. Still, murder has a way of doing that sometimes, she thought.

"Elise," Morgana hissed through the keyhole. The ghost stopped moving and looked toward her. "Elise, what are you doing?"

Elise put her head right through the door and looked

down at Morgana in confusion. "Why are you kneeling on the floor outside my room?" The ghost asked, sounding now more irritated than upset.

"Because the door's locked, and I can't get through it like you can."

Elise just looked confused.

"You do realise that you're dead, Elise?" Morgana said, in as regretful a tone as she could manage.

"Don't be ridiculous. And why can't I get through this doorway?" She seemed to be straining against it, but though her head was out, the rest of her body refused to follow it.

"I'm sorry, I don't know. I suspect you are stuck in that room for the moment." The rules that governed ghosts often made no sense to Morgana, but it was rare that they could wander freely, usually being tied to the place where they'd died. "Elise, you were killed last night. Do you see the blood?"

"There's no blood, what are you talking about?" Elise's head vanished back into the room.

"On the bed? Is there blood on the bed?" Morgana persisted, knowing she would probably have to jog the ghost's memories. They always struggled with remembering things properly, as though half their mind had already moved on. It was an aspect of ghosts that Morgana found particularly annoying.

"There's no blood on my bed. No sheets either. Where is my bedding? Drat that girl!" Elise moved about the room and Morgana went back down to the keyhole. It occurred to her that the police had probably taken the bedding away. She squinted at the figure inside. Elise was in a nightdress, something that might have been blue if she wasn't so transparent, and elegantly long with lace at the shoulders.

"Look at your nightdress Elise, it's torn and soaked with blood, do you see?"

There was a shriek from inside as the ghost registered the state of her clothing. "My nightdress! It's ruined! Mary?" Elise raised her voice. "Mary? Where is that stupid girl?"

"Who's Mary?" Morgana asked.

"My maid. A lazy stupid lump."

"I thought your maid was called Bonny?"

There was a long pause and Morgana sighed with frustration. That was something else she'd forgotten about ghosts. They had absolutely no concept of time. It became all muddled up for them, which was good in the sense that they didn't really feel it passing, but bad because it meant they were useless at keeping in the present moment.

"Oh, yes, Bonny. I saw to Mary, making eyes at my husband when I wasn't there. She took her own life in the end."

"She committed suicide? Or did you do something to her, Elise?" Morgana tried to keep the anger out of her voice. She was beginning to wonder how many more skeletons there were in the woman's closet and if the death of this Mary could be yet another motive for murder.

Elise however, had lost interest, and Morgana could only just see her moving about again, trying to open drawers and peering under the bed.

"Mary?" Elise called again. "Where did you hide my pills? I can't sleep, I need them."

Morgana sat back on her heels. Having a coherent conversation with a ghost was an effort at the best of times, but trying to do it through a keyhole was even harder.

"Elise," she called out firmly. "Please try to think. It's really important. Do you have any idea who murdered you?"

The ghost stopped moving and appeared to be thinking. "I was sleeping. I can't remember anything. But *why* was I sleeping, I didn't take my pills! Somebody's moved them now. I need them back, where are they?" Elise resumed her search.

Morgana shook her head and rose stiffly back to her feet. Elise wasn't going to be able to answer the question.

"Who are you talking to?"

Morgana turned and saw Georgie coming up the stairs. "Just to myself." She said, with a fake laugh.

"Who are you talking to?" Elise's head popped through the door again.

Morgana gave a silent sigh and decided to ignore the dead in favour of the living. "Is dinner over?" she asked Georgie.

"Yes, come back down and have a drinkie, you look like you need one. I was just going to refresh my lipstick, then let's hit the liquor cabinet, hmm? You just missed Keefe's big announcement. I actually thought I was getting somewhere with him but he'd just told the whole table that he's gay. Bad news for women everywhere, but good news for men, I suppose."

Judy will not be pleased he's outed himself! She thought, feeling her spirits lift on Keefe's behalf. "Why not, I suddenly find I'm not as tired as I thought," Morgana agreed, and allowed herself to be herded back to the house-party. *Who knows, perhaps I'll learn something more if I hang around and keep my eyes and ears open.*

Chapter Nineteen

For the second night running, Morgana lay awake unable to sleep. She hadn't managed to learn anything more and she was getting disheartened. Tristan had made her feel like a real detective, as though she actually contributed something to the investigation, but so far she really hadn't added much at all. She was basically just a regular person who could sometimes see people's moods. A human lie detector at best.

She roamed around her bedroom for a while trying to think through everybody's statements that day and see where they might have missed something, but in the end, she knew that with so much on her mind she was unlikely to get to sleep for a while and eventually decided that she would go back downstairs to the library and choose something to read.

She opened her bedroom door tentatively, taking time to look up and down the corridor, but there was none of the bustle of the night before and everything was silent.

As she crept down the stairs she noticed that there were still lamps lit in the hall, and lights on in the larger and the more cozy drawing rooms as she passed through them, which told her that she probably wasn't the only one still awake.

She paused for a long moment outside the door of the library, feeling convinced that there was someone inside, and not at all sure that she wanted to encounter whoever it was. However, she had come downstairs for a reason and she might as well see it through. She tapped twice on the library door out of politeness before pushing it open, just in case it was more than one person inside. But as she stepped in she saw that only one armchair was currently in use.

Lord Latheborne was sitting beside the fire reading and he looked up, saw it was her, and scowled.

Morgana sighed quietly to herself.

"I'm sorry to disturb your peace," she said, trying not to allow an irritated tone into her voice. "But would it be okay if I borrowed a book to read, just for tonight? I'm finding it rather hard to get to sleep."

Lord Latheborne's expression lost a little of its hardness and he closed his book. "I'm sure you're not the only one feeling that way tonight. The event this morning was rather unexpected, wasn't it?"

He extended a hand towards the chair opposite him and she gave him a quizzical look before settling into it. She hadn't intended to get into further conversation with anyone but on the other hand, it was a good opportunity to question him more informally and also to perhaps get to the bottom of why he was so antagonistic towards her.

She also couldn't help being strongly drawn to him somehow. He had a strong but quiet presence and she felt calm around him, there was no pretence in him and it was strangely pleasant to be with someone who hid very little and simply expressed their feelings without her ever needing to read him to see what he wasn't saying.

"You look very sweet in your pj's," he said, as though picking up on the intimacy of her thoughts. "Somehow much better than in your fancy day clothes."

"That almost sounds like a compliment."

"It is."

There was a silence as he looked into her eyes, and she had a feeling he was thinking about kissing her, but then he suddenly cleared his throat and drew back a little.

"Is it a good book, my lord?" she asked, trying for a safe topic of conversation.

He smiled slightly and shook his head. "No, it's an extremely boring book on sheep farming, and I think that perhaps now might be the time to drop all the title stuff between us, wouldn't you say? It seems silly when we're sat here in the middle of the night."

Morgana raised her eyebrows. "You're being friendly to me. Have I done something to redeem myself?"

She noticed his eyes slide away from her, and onto a magazine that lay on a nearby side table. She followed his look and saw her own face staring out of the page under the bolded title of *The relationships and rise of Morwenna Emrys.* Morgana jumped to her feet and snatched it up, while he looked embarrassed.

She ignored his small protest and began to scan it, her lip twisting in disgust as she read. *Morwenna, sometimes known as 'the wisteria' of the theatre world, seems to get bigger roles as she gets more influential boyfriends. Her social-climbing at a rapid rate could certainly be accounted for by her taste in men as opposed to her talents as an actress, and she discards them as fast as she acquires them, leaving a string of broken hearts in her wake.*

There followed a series of photographs of Morwenna eating out with various men, or coming out of nightclubs on their arm, and ended with a picture of her and Ethan kissing in a doorway.

It continued: *Almost ten years older than Ethan Cope, who is a good two decades younger than her previous beau, it would appear that her sudden interest in the much younger man was more down to his recent Oscar win than his not inconsiderable good looks.*

"I'm *seven years* older than Ethan," she said, furious on Morwenna's behalf.

"It's still quite a gap," Lord Latheborne said, almost apologetically.

She narrowed her eyes on him. "How old are you? 34, 35?"

He gave a small, suspicious nod.

"I'm twenty-eight, so that makes you seven years older than me. Would anyone, even for a moment, consider you much too old for me?"

Lord Latheborne gave a rueful smile. "I suppose that's true. Somehow it seems more acceptable. Perhaps it is rather unfair on women that it doesn't seem so normal the other way around. On the other hand, it's difficult to think of Ethan as anything more than a boy at twenty-one, whereas we are both all grown up." He had a slight twinkle in his eye as he said it, and she found herself rolling her eyes, all her anger draining out of her.

Morgana looked again at the article. At least now she knew where Judy had seen the picture of Morwenna with a fringe cut in. And her sister certainly did seem to have been dating a lot of high profile men over the course of the last year. She couldn't entirely blame Lord Latheborne for thinking the worst of Morwenna, but still, it rankled that he'd judged her based on one article in a stupid magazine.

"Don't always believe everything you read," she tossed the magazine aside.

"No, you're quite right. I had it in my head that all

actors were generally deceitful. After all, their job is fooling you into believing in their portrayal of a character. But you're not like that, are you? I like how direct and honest you are."

She softened under his gaze. "Thank you, Oliver." She had a go at using his given name, seeing as he'd suggested she should, and found she was at ease with it. It was a nice name. She was about to tell him the whole truth, that she wasn't actually Morwenna at all, and hoped he wouldn't hate her for the previous pretence, but he cut her off before she could speak.

"However, Morwenna, I'm still uncomfortable about your relationship with Ethan. He's very green behind the ears and however close the age gap between you, I'd be failing in my duty to him if I didn't say you really do seem much too mature for him."

Her hackles instantly raised again and she got to her feet. "There is no relationship between Ethan and myself, but you have no duty to me, and so I shall feel free to tell you to stick your opinions up your arse, *my lord.*" And with that, she grabbed the nearest book and flounced out.

It was only as she reached the formal drawing room and saw the ghost there that she stopped. She looked at the book she was holding and read the title. *Positions and duties in a large household.* It had a picture of a maid carrying a breakfast tray on the front. She suddenly realised the question that she *should* have asked Elise, and hurried toward the stairs to do so immediately.

Morgana had just reached the landing when all the lights went out.

"Batwing!" she cursed, nearly smacking right into the

wall in the sudden darkness. She reached out a hand to steady herself in position so she didn't accidentally blunder straight down the stairs again when she heard a cry, then a series of thumping noises, and then running footsteps. She spun wildly on the spot trying to get her bearings of where it was coming from.

"Poppy!" she yelled loudly, absolutely convinced that something awful had just happened.

"Where are you, Morgana? I can't see a thing. Damn it!" Poppy's voice came from the hall below, including the sound of china breaking as Poppy clearly blundered into something.

Then a door opened somewhere downstairs and she saw Lord Latheborne coming through it with a candelabra in hand.

"Is it another power cut?" Georgie's voice sounded somewhere close to Morgana.

"No," Lord Latheborne called up to them. "Wrong weather for a power cut, it must be a fuse or something. I'm going to the fuse box now, everyone just stay where you are." He disappeared into the dining room and they were in darkness once again.

Time seemed to move incredibly slowly suddenly, and Morgana found she was holding her breath in the silence, straining her ears for movement. She heard a couple of doors open around the gallery and Ethan's voice saying, "I really must learn to keep a candle in my bedroom, this is getting ridiculous."

"Is it normal?" Keefe's accented tone floated out.

"Not really," Ethan answered, "but it does happen sometimes in a storm."

"There isn't a storm," Georgie's voice added.

Then the lights came on again.

Morgana didn't hesitate; she was running to where the initial cry had come from and found herself heading for the stairs to the tower.

Just as she'd dreaded there was someone lying at the bottom. "Poppy!" She yelled, going down beside the figure and rolling them toward her. But she already knew who it was, only Judy would be wearing a flowery dressing-gown like that.

"Oh crumbs," Poppy arrived at Morgana's side. "Is she?"

"Dead? Yes." Morgana checked Judy's pulse, but she didn't really need to. Judy's eyes were staring lifelessly at the ceiling and blood trickled slowly from the crushed side of her head.

Chapter Twenty-one

Poppy took very little time to assess the scene and to herd them all into the dining room, where she insisted that every member of the household be awoken and present. She also went around checking all doors to the outside and ascertaining that they were still locked.

Louise was the only one who wasn't there, but nobody was surprised by this as they knew she slept in a different building. Georgie looked ravishing and still wore a full face of makeup, and Lord Latheborne was still dressed, but everyone else was in their night-clothes and Mrs Brown even had curlers in her hair and a face mask on.

"I don't want anyone to leave this room," Poppy said, firmly. "DI Lowen and DS Treharne are on their way."

Georgie leaned in close to Morgana. "Are you of the same mind as me that it's unlikely there are *two* murderers in this house?"

Morgana nodded. "Which means it definitely wasn't Harvey or Kitty. It was someone at this table." They both began to scan the table, but nobody stood out as looking particularly guilty. The only person showing emotion was Bernie. Or rather, a total lack of emotion. He was staring into space, clearly too shocked to move or speak.

"He looks so lost," Georgie whispered, "but it seems really inappropriate for me to offer comfort right now."

"I know what you mean," Morgana muttered back, "and it would also make you look really guilty. Who would want his wife out the way more?"

Georgie's eyes widened. "That's true, and I stand to benefit from Elise's death too! I'm going to get her part in the historical drama."

"I don't think it was you if that's any consolation." Morgana was actually fairly sure of this. She had taken the time on the way down the stairs to catch hold of Georgie's arm and try to read her. She hadn't had much of a chance, but the skin to skin contact had been enough to convince Morgana that Georgie hadn't just done something really evil. Of course, she also knew that her senses weren't infallible.

If I could just open my third eye, she thought. *But I can't risk it here in front of everyone. But maybe when Tristan gets here? He'd keep me safe, both from others and from totally collapsing.*

As if on cue, Aiden Lowen and Tristan came through the door. Aiden's sharp eyes swept the group.

"We're going to look over the crime scene. Everyone stay here, please." Then they were gone again and everyone sat in silence, waiting.

They reappeared about ten minutes later. "DS Treharne, you'll wait here. PC Dunn, you will brief me in the library." Aiden Lowen said gruffly, then stomped away again, followed by Poppy.

Morgana immediately approached Tristan. "I was thinking it might be time for me to open my third eye?" she said, getting straight to the point.

He shook his head. "Not right now, it takes you too long to recover. The DI is going to want to talk to you next."

"Of course. I assume you have come to the same conclusion as us that Harvey and Kitty probably didn't kill Elise?"

"Unfortunately, yes. We also know where the pills came from now." He kept his voice very low.

"You do? Who?"

Tristan's eyes travelled the room and came to rest on Keefe.

"Really?" Morgana bit her lip, unconvinced. "He didn't have any real motive for either murder, not anymore."

"That you know of," Tristan replied. "But I didn't say it was him."

They both turned as the door opened and Poppy came back in. "Miss Emrys? The Inspector wants you."

Morgana gave a nod of acknowledgment, and looked back to Tristan. "Then who?"

"I can't say right now, go." He gave her a little push toward the door and Morgana went, throwing him a look of annoyance.

She found Detective Inspector Lowen in the library.

"*Two* more murders, Morgana," he said dryly, by way of greeting. He'd questioned her before when they'd crossed path over a totally different death.

"I know, just unlucky I guess." She shrugged apologetically.

"Or very lucky. Tristan thinks Judy was murdered because she knew something. It's a good thing the murderer doesn't think you do too, wouldn't you say?"

Morgana ignored the last comment. "I agree with Tristan. Judy was hinting at knowing something, and Tristan *warned* her it would be dangerous to withhold information. I just wish she'd listened to him! Do you think she tried to approach the murderer herself?"

He gave a brief incline of his head. "That's exactly

what we think. From what I can gather from the statements she was in the habit of 'collecting secrets', maybe she thought to leverage this one? Now, tell me what you saw and heard, I believe you were actually out in the hall when it happened?"

"I was on my way back from the library, I'd been to get a book." She decided not to mention that she'd stopped on the way back to talk to a ghost. "I was outside Elise's bedroom when the lights went out. I heard a cry, then Judy tumbling down the stairs from the tower, and then footsteps running."

"Where did they go?"

Morgana screwed up her face, trying to remember. "They came down from the tower, and kept going down, I think. But they didn't go past me, so they can't have gone down the stairs, so maybe along the corridor away from me?"

"To the bedrooms, you mean? Or perhaps down a different set of stairs?"

"Yes," she said, unsure. "But there aren't any other stairs."

"There are. There's a door near the tower and stairs that go down to the servants quarters."

"Oh," Morgana was surprised by that, but then, there was so much of the house that she still hadn't explored.

"Do you think that might tally with what you heard? Someone going down another set of stairs?"

"Yes," she said again, very hesitantly. "It could have been." She thought for another moment. "Keefe, Ethan, and Georgie came out of their rooms, and none of their voices sounded breathless. I'd have thought whoever was running would sound out of breath?" She offered.

"Which leaves Bernie, Lord Latheborne, and the servants." He seemed to agree with her. "And yourself, of course."

Once again she chose to ignore his last comment. "I saw Bernie come out of his bedroom after the lights came on, which he couldn't have reached except by going right past me. And Lord Latheborne was down in the library, he couldn't have come up the stairs to kill Judy without me seeing him." A horrible thought struck her. "Oh, except I suppose someone had to be downstairs to turn out the lights. Do you think it was two people in on it together?"

"No. The fuse was blown from the music room. Someone tipped a glass of water over the light switch. It tripped out the whole house."

She was relieved it wasn't Latheborne, unless of course he'd somehow had time to run up the servants stairs, go to the tower, meet Judy, trip the lights, murder her and run all the way back down to the library? She shook her head decisively, it just wasn't possible.

"Who would know how to do that? And that it would work?" Morgana asked.

"Someone familiar with the house," Aiden said, gruffly.

"Or someone with a theatrical background?" she suggested. "They must work with lights and what-not all the time?"

"No. We have a pretty good idea now, and your version of the events tallies with it perfectly. Thank you for your time."

He rose from his chair and went back to the dining

room with Morgana following at his heels. When he reached the room he took out a pair of handcuffs.

"Carlton Adams, you're under arrest for the murders of Elise Everett and Judy Gossard."

Chapter Twenty-two

Morgana sat back in her dining chair watching with horror and confusion as Tristan read Adams his rights. It just didn't make sense.

Lord Latheborne began protesting loudly, and even Keefe tried to intervene, but a few sharp words from the Inspector had them both soon silenced.

Adams himself didn't say anything. He just stood there, apparently stunned and tears swimming in his eyes. He looked like anything but a murderer.

"Miss Santos." The Inspector turned to Bonny, who'd been sitting quietly by the door to the kitchen and trying to fade into the wallpaper since they'd all been summoned out of bed. "You will accompany us back to the station, we have a few questions for you too. PC Dunn, can you escort Miss Santos please?" DI Lowen announced as he led Adams out into the hall. "DS Treharne, I'll leave you to secure the scene, the forensics team will be here at first light. Stay put until then."

Tristan nodded and went up the stairs, leaving everyone else still sitting in the dining room, not quite sure what to do with themselves.

Georgie couldn't wait any longer, she rushed over to Bernie's side and put her arms around him. He buried his head into her midriff and finally broke down, beginning to cry loudly. "What am I going to do?" he wailed.

"I'm gonna take care of you, love, you don't need to do anythin' at all right now, see?" Georgie said firmly. Morgana noticed that Georgie's posh accent had fallen away and she sounded like a born and bred Londoner suddenly. She put her shoulder under his arm and lifted him to his feet. "I'm taking Bernie for a stiff drink. Anyone else need one?"

"I do." Ethan followed her. Keefe stayed where he was, looking distressed by the turn of events. Morgana felt very sorry for him. She didn't know how serious his dalliance with Adams had been, as they'd only just met, but he seemed pretty cut up about it.

Lord Latheborne put a hand to his head. "I need tea, gallons of tea. Would you mind, Mrs Brown?"

"Course not, y'lordship." Mrs Brown jumped to her feet, and seemed very glad of an excuse to leave the room too.

Morgana put her head down on the table, feeling suddenly very tired. She hadn't been to bed yet and she could hear the clock in the hall chiming 3 am. But her brain refused to let her rest. So much didn't add up for her.

Yes, she could see the logic that the pills had belonged to Keefe and that Adams had therefore had easy access to them. She thought back to what Bonny had said when they'd questioned her; Bonny had actually seen Adams going back down the stairs just before she'd discovered the murder. But *why?* Judy's murder made more sense if Judy had known and tried to blackmail him or something? Still, the motive was missing for the first death.

Morgana got to her feet and went to find Tristan. He was covering Judy's body over and a camera lay by his feet.

"What do you know about Adams that we don't?" she said, getting straight to the point.

Tristan heaved a long-suffering sigh. "We run background checks on everyone, Morgana, *all* the way back. Not that we've been very successful with all of them as yet, these acting lot tend to change their names, which confuses things. But Adams was easy. His mother left shortly after he was born and he was raised by his father in England, but his mother was Spanish. She returned to Spain and had another child. Would you like to guess who his half-sister is?"

Morgana's mouth dropped open. "Bonny? Seriously? I never picked up on anything between them."

"But people don't tend to see the servants much, do they? Their job is to be unobtrusive. It's an acting talent all of its own. She came into Elise's employment *after* this trip was planned, Elise has had it in her diary for seven months to the week, and she took Bonny on *six* months ago. Coincidence, or, well planned by Bonny and Adams? We are just guessing, but I'd say that Elise probably had something on Bonny, and she turned to her brother for help dealing with it."

"You don't think she was involved in the murder?"

"Maybe. But he was the one who had access to the Amoxin that was used, and he knows the house and the fact that just one wet light would trip out the main fuse. I suspect she'll be charged as an accessory." Tristan spread his hands. "We got them, that's what matters."

"I didn't see it, I didn't see any sign of it in their auras." Morgana couldn't shake the niggling feeling she had that there was something she'd missed, but it had come from someone else.

Tristan put a hand on her shoulder. "You did good, it was helpful. You won't always be able to simply point at a murderer and say *he did it*, and that's okay."

"Gee, thanks." She frowned at him, feeling patronised, even though she knew he didn't mean it that way. She walked away and went to her bedroom, thinking that she might as well lie down for a few hours of rest. No doubt the arrival of the forensics team would make sleep impossible as soon as it was morning.

She was just drifting off into a fitful slumber when she sat bolt upright again. She still hadn't spoken to Elise and asked her the obvious question: Who was it that brought her the hot chocolate?

Chapter Twenty-three

Five minutes later, filled with new knowledge, Morgana was running back to Tristan where he still knelt at the bottom of the tower.

"Can you gather everyone again? I know who the real murderer is. Judy told us!" She said breathlessly, all tiredness now gone.

"Wait, what? She didn't say...oh no, you don't mean to tell me that she's here *in spirit* do you?" Tristan rubbed his temples as if he were suddenly getting a headache and Morgana was the cause.

"No. At least, I haven't seen her. It was *before*; she dropped massive hints, but we didn't pick up on it. So, can you do it?"

"Fine, I'm just finished. But please don't put us on a wild goose chase Morgana, this has been traumatic enough for everyone here."

It was another fifteen minutes before everyone left in the house was once again assembled in the dining room.

"What's going on?" Georgie looked annoyed.

"I'm sorry, it's my fault," Morgana said, not sitting down. "But a few things fell into place for me this evening. As some of you know, from when DS Treharne questioned you, I do sometimes help the police with investigations. This isn't because I have any special knowledge, but simply because I'm sometimes more perceptive, yet in this case, I haven't been at all." She gave an apologetic smile, but no one smiled back.

Morgana gave an inward sigh and continued. "You see, everything we needed to know was actually revealed to us, but we didn't put any of it together. Judy told us a story about Elise, slipped into other stories, about the time Elise pushed a lovely young actress off a balcony and broke her back. Her name was Sarah Finch," Morgana paused for dramatic effect, "and she murdered Elise!"

Everyone looked around the table in confusion, their eyes finally resting on Georgie.

"It's not me!" Georgie protested.

"No, it's not. But you have changed your name, haven't you? It was pointed out to me that many actors do. Keefe?" Morgana looked at him.

He gave a grudging nod.

"And me," Ethan said with a boyish smile. "My real name is Ethan Copstead-Latheborne, but it was a bit of a mouthful. Ethan Cope has a better ring to it."

"I think Sarah Finch did the same thing, she decided her real name was too boring and changed it for a while. Prior to that she called Brown, or Mrs Brown to us."

Mrs. Brown lifted her head, looking insulted. "'Ere now, what are you implying?"

The eyes of everyone else went to Mrs Brown, seated by the door to the kitchen, then back to Morgana in confusion.

"I'm implying that you are, in fact, Sarah Finch. Elise didn't recognise you, she was too self-obsessed, and Bernie didn't take much notice of the staff. But Judy, she was extremely observant, I suspect she knew who you were right from the start, but she liked keeping secrets. It was you who dropped the plate of pheasant when she made the comment about people changing their name and pretending to be someone else, wasn't it?"

"That's ridiculous," Mrs. Brown said, firmly.

"I'm sorry, I'm confused," Lord Latheborne put in. "Mrs Brown hardly qualifies as a *lovely young* actress."

"But she could," Morgana continued. "I thought Georgie was about fifteen years younger than her real age when we met, and the effect could easily be done in reverse. It's called makeup. It's probably the reason she's got a face-pack on now. It was Bonny who told us that Mrs. Brown wore a great deal of makeup and pretended to be older than she was. Bonny thought she was pretending to be weak to get others to do her work for her, but you really *do* have a bad back, don't you?"

"'Course I do!" Mrs. Brown said, rubbing it.

Morgana looked at her sympathetically. "How long were you in that wheelchair? The doctors said you'd never walk again, but you proved them wrong, didn't you? And you kept track of Elise, where she was going, and waited for an opportunity. I think Lord Latheborne said you'd been here about six months? That timing would fit with coming shortly after Elise signed to be here. And who would suspect you? The whole thing happened in America, I assume. You're an excellent actress, but your dialect isn't quite right, you speak like someone from the South-East of England, but called me 'duck' which is generally only used in North."

"Stuff and piffle, you can't prove any of this. So what if I look a bit older than my birth certificate says I am, I've 'ad an 'ardlife!"

Georgie stared at Mrs. Brown. "The correct saying is *stuff and nonsense.* Nobody's used *piffle* in England for centuries."

Tristan had stood very still, taking it all in, but now

he looked at Morgana expectantly. "Anything else? We can go into all this of course, but it's hardly conclusive."

"I'm assuming you got a background on Mrs. Brown, but there were some gaps in it?" she asked him.

Tristan nodded slowly.

"And Mrs. Brown had keys to everyone's bedrooms," Morgana continued. "I don't know when she took the Amoxin from Keefe's room, but that's the beauty of being Housekeeper isn't it? She can come and go without suspicion. She also knew the house well enough to fuse out the lights. And it was Mrs Brown who took Elise the poisoned hot chocolate. Elise wasn't the type to make it for herself, and it wasn't Bonny or Adams, so who else could it have been? And there was no cup at the scene, whoever stabbed her cleared it away. The teacups are a set, aren't they? I bet it was washed up and simply replaced with the others."

"You've no proof of any of this!" Mrs. Brown stated.

"No physical evidence as yet," Tristan agreed. "But I think there's enough to go on to take you in for questioning. It's only a matter of time before we fill in where you've been for the last few years, and we can get medical records that will show us if you've been in an accident and prove if you are, in fact, also Sarah Finch." He moved towards her but she scuttled away.

"It's all Judy's fault!" She spat out, her accent going seamlessly from British to American. "She could have just minded her own business, she said she didn't care about Elise's death, but she wanted me to go back to work in acting as if I'd ever set foot in that poisoned paradise again! She said she owned me now. But no one tells me what I can and can't do, I proved them all wrong. Five years I was in that wheelchair, but I was stronger than any doctor believed I could be." She waved her arms about madly and Tristan had to duck around her to restrain her. In the end, he decided to cuff her, but she kept ranting as she was led from the room, and they could all still hear her tirade as she was marched out of the house.

There was collective blowing out of breath as some of the tension left the room along with Mrs. Brown.

"So, it was her all along." Keefe shook his head in bewilderment.

"I'd say that was a confession," Morgana agreed.

"Well, I feel rather sorry for her," Georgie said, "Elise ruined her life."

"I don't," Lord Latheborne said, looking rather sick. "She's obviously insane, and a cold-blooded killer, and I've been living under the same roof as her for months! Supposing I'd complained about the food?"

Chapter Twenty-four

This time when Morgana went up to her bedroom, she knew she'd have no trouble sleeping at all. She stopped, though, on the way up to peer through the keyhole into Elise's bedroom. It was quiet and empty. Morgana nodded to herself. Elise's spirit would know they'd caught her real murderer and so she'd moved on. Which was how it should be.

She fell into bed and didn't even awake when the forensics team came and removed Judy's body.

The daylight outside was bright as midday when she eventually yawned and stretched, and looking at her watch, she saw that she'd slept right through until almost lunch. The house was eerily silent as she went to the bathroom to shower and dress, and took a few extra minutes to pack her bags before she braved going downstairs.

She poked her head into the dining room, fully expecting it to be empty, as no big Sunday roast would be occurring that day now, and discovered the Baroness sitting there eating a pork pie.

"I need Salad Cream," The Baroness told her, before squinting at Morgana in recognition. "Oh, it's you. Well, that's alright I suppose. More tolerable than the rest of them."

Morgana smothered a laugh at this high praise. "I'm leaving shortly, but can I get the Salad Cream for you before I go, Baroness?"

"Condiment cupboard, over there." The lady pointed a bony finger, and Morgana retrieved it for her. "You don't have to leave," she said between dollops as she totally covered the pork pie. "You have my blessing to marry him if you want to."

This time Morgana laughed out loud. She had no idea who the Baroness was referring to, probably either Lord Latheborne or Ethan, but it didn't matter. She had no intention of marrying anyone at all in the near future. She left the room, still laughing, and tried the formal drawing room instead. To her surprise she found Tristan, occupying an armchair and reading a newspaper.

"Hello, you're still here?" she said, sinking down on an embroidered chaise, which turned out to be far more uncomfortable than it looked.

"I wanted to tell you that Mrs. Brown gave a full statement. She's pleading insanity, but she did indeed stab Elise, and murder Judy too."

"I know," Morgana said, smothering another yawn.

"And to thank you, of course. Especially as we'd already arrested three of the wrong people!" he said, tutting to himself.

"You'd have got her eventually, all those paper trails you chase, I've no doubt you'd have worked it out soon enough. Plus, I had the help of a ghost. It was Elise who told me that Mrs. Brown had given her the hot chocolate, it just all fell into place once I knew that."

"Well, there you are then." Tristan looked satisfied. "There's no way I could have got information from a ghost. But you're right, we'd have discovered it the old fashioned way in the end. The crux here was discovering the true murderer in time, she could have left the country at any moment, and then it would have been much harder, so, we really do appreciate your help in catching her quickly."

"In that case, you're welcome," Morgana said. "What happened with Harvey and Kitty, did they come back here?"

He shook his head. "They went straight to a hotel yesterday morning. Probably needed some alone time. I believe Adams packed up their things before he left today."

"Adams is gone?" Morgana became more alert with surprise.

"Keefe collected him and Bonny from the station several hours ago. Apparently, he's asked Adams to go back to America with him."

"As his butler?"

"No." Tristan laughed at her brightening expression. "They also took Bonny, so Adams can get to know her better. Apparently Adams and Bonny had no idea they were related, it was just one of those weird coincidences."

"Ha," Morgana scoffed. "I'll bet my witchy hat that Bonny knew. She'll bleed them both dry if they let her."

"Well, if anyone can get her on the straight and narrow then it's probably Adams, he really does have the most spotless reputation."

"Until he was arrested for murder," she pointed out, getting in a dig at Tristan.

"Yes, well, the least said about that the better. It did seem to fit all the facts though. Ghost witnesses aside."

Morgana looked over to the fireplace where the ghost of a serving girl in Victorian garb still tended to the fire. "I wonder if I should offer to do something about the ghosts here, do you think Lord Latheborne would believe me if I told him he's got a couple of them knocking about?"

"You'll have to ask him yourself. He's in the library I think. Probably exhausted from all the houseguests and murder, and seeing everyone off today. Georgie and Bernie have gone too. Georgie left a letter for you, I think, and Bernie said something about seeing you on-set."

"He'll see *Morwenna*, not me ever again, I hope! Though I might keep in touch with Georgie and I suspect the two of them will make a go of it."

"About Morwenna." Tristan cleared his throat awkwardly. "I did want to clear something up with you. Remember when I kissed you?"

"Yes." She tried not to blush.

"You asked me how I knew you weren't Morwenna, well, it was what you said just before. You said that every time we made love I begged for more."

Morgana shifted uncomfortably. "I was just being silly."

"The thing is, whatever Morwenna might have told you in the past, she and I...We never did. I wanted you to know that."

Morgana stared at him. "But Morwenna doesn't lie. Wait, she didn't ever actually *say* it." Morgana was talking more to herself now. "She just implied it, which isn't the same at all." She fixed her eyes on his. "How come? You were together for over a year, and seemed really into each other."

"She was *fifteen* when we got together, Morgana. I was eighteen and stupid, but I wasn't *that* stupid! Maybe if we'd stayed a couple for longer, but we broke up not long after your sixteenth birthday. My whole relationship with her wasn't much more than kissing, and even that was years and years ago now. I don't know if that means anything, or changes anything?" He tailed off, regarding her with an unreadable expression.

Morgana sensed rather than saw the flickering of desire in his aura, and she knew her own would match it. She wanted to open her abilities and bask in it. It was for *her,* not Morwenna. But instead, she pulled back slightly.

"I...I don't know. If you're talking about you and me, then I'm not sure that it does. You were still my sister's boyfriend."

He gave her a tight smile and got to his feet. "Probably for the best. Now, I'd better be off, especially now I know there are ghosts all around us."

She too stood up, disappointment coursing through her at how it could have been different if she'd just said yes.

"I'll see you soon though?" *Ridiculous sexual tension and all*, she added silently.

"You will, there's bound to be another murder sooner or later where you're concerned." He leaned forward and gave her a quick kiss on the cheek, before striding out into the hall.

Morgana expelled a long breath. "Speaking of which, I suppose I'd better find my host and say goodbye." She went through the door to the informal drawing room and stopped outside the library. She decided not to knock this time and went in.

"Miss Emrys." Lord Latheborne rose from his chair as she entered. "Miss *Morgana* Emrys, I believe."

"Oh dear, are you angry?" She regarded him warily, unsure how he had taken the news. "Who told you?"

"Ethan and I had a conversation this morning. I admit I was angry at first, I had come to think better of you than such deception. But he assured me it would have been Morwenna's idea and that you were only being a good sister. After thinking it over, I've decided that I'm rather glad you're you and not her."

"Oh? Because you have such a low opinion of actresses?"

"Because it means you don't have any relationship with my nephew, and I'm free to invite you for dinner."

"Invite me for dinner?" She found herself repeating his words out of sheer surprise.

"Yes, it would give me a chance to get to know the *real* you." He looked amused at her expression. "But not here though, I suddenly find myself rather short of staff, and with no housekeeper and no butler, well…I suppose I could always make spaghetti bolognaise. I'm afraid I haven't done much real cooking since my University days. A restaurant makes more sense, I think. But perhaps you can't forgive me for my previous rudeness?"

"I forgive you, Oliver. After all, I should apologise for my deception too."

"Good, then we can start over by having dinner. Except, you haven't actually given me any indication of whether you might want to yet?"

Morgana glanced out the window and watched as Tristan's car disappeared down the driveway.

"Yes," she said, after a moment of thought. "I think I'd like that very much."

~

Books in this series

Murder Most Pumpkin (prequel)
Body at the Bakery
Killer at the Castle
Murder at the Mansion

www.stellaberrybooks.com

In honour of Morgana's love of crosswords (and mine), I always like to include one. Have a go! It's a good test of memory, but do let me know if you'd like them to be harder ☺

www.stellaberrybooks.com/contact

Murder at the Mansion Crossword

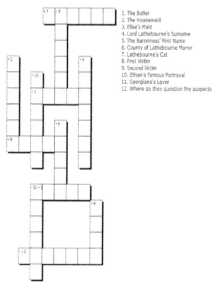

1. The Butler
2. The Housemaid
3. Elise's Maid
4. Lord Lathebourne's Surname
5. The Baronness' First Name
6. County of Lathebourne Manor
7. Lathebourne's Cat
8. First Victim
9. Second Victim
10. Ethan's Famous Portrayal
11. Georgiana's Lover
12. Where do they question the suspects

The solution will be posted to my Reader Group *secret* page on my website

(Sign up to join via the link in my books, or directly on my website)

Printed in Great Britain
by Amazon